Tamar, Erika.

Out of control

OUT OF CONTROL

BOOKS BY ERIKA TAMAR

It Happened at Cecilia's
Out of Control

OUT OF CONTROL

ERIKA TAMAR

ATHENEUM 1991 NEW YORK

Maxwell Macmillan Canada *Toronto*
Maxwell Macmillan International
New York Oxford Singapore Sydney

Atheneum
Macmillan Publishing Company
866 Third Avenue
New York, NY 10022

Maxwell Macmillan Canada, Inc.
1200 Eglinton Avenue East
Suite 200
Don Mills, Ontario M3C 3N1

Macmillan Publishing Company is part of the Maxwell Communication Group of Companies.

First edition
Printed in the United States of America
1 2 3 4 5 6 7 8 9 10
Designed by Kimberly M. Hauck

Library of Congress Cataloging-in-Publication Data

Tamar, Erika,
Out of control/Erika Tamar.—1st ed.
p. cm.
Summary: A talented singer's love turns to obsession when he starts dating the female guitarist in his rock band.
ISBN 0-689-31689-5
[1. Bands (Music)—Fiction. 2. Friendship—Fiction.] I. Title.
PZ7.T1,590u 1991 91–4973
[Fic]—dc20.

For Monica

Once they were five. They formed a tight knot that was more than the sum of its five strands. Now there are only four and their lives have unraveled.

It is one of those perfect Long Island beginning-of-fall mornings. The damp mugginess of summer is finally gone and the trees are just beginning to turn color. The grass of this cemetery is immaculately groomed, as velvet smooth as the golf course. The terrain is gently hilly around the well-trimmed graves. The Boulevard is hidden by strategically placed shrubbery and the whir of traffic is muted. Suggestions of sudden death or violence or madness would be tasteless in so perfect a setting.

There is the group of mourners—family and relatives and friends—and there is the droning voice of someone officiating at the grave site.

It is an obscenely bright day, complete with sky-blue sky.

The four of them are standing apart from the rest of the group, almost touching, huddled together against the assault of the sun. They avoid each other's eyes. Nothing will ever be the same again. Nothing can ever roll it back to the way it was at the beginning. . . .

Jessica

I have a feeling we're all very crazy.

It's a beautiful Friday night in May and we should be out someplace, enjoying the spring air and no-school-tomorrow. Instead, we're all hunched over in Darren's damp basement because we've let him browbeat us into rehearsing for hours and hours.

Mike must be thinking the same thing. He just leaned over and said, under his breath, "Darren's getting out of control."

"Yeah, really," I said. Darren is just about the most self-possessed guy I've ever seen.

Out of Control is the name of the group because that's our signature song; it's the catchiest one Darren ever wrote. It's funny that the kids like it for all the wrong reasons. Darren meant it in a satirical way; he was commenting on the people in this town not really liking kids, seeing them as potentially menacing, shades of *A Clockwork Orange*. So the chorus is all this cliché stuff: "Out of control, rampant and amok . . ." The way Johnny sings it, though, the dangerous look on his face, the way he raises and shakes his fist, makes it into something else. The kids raise their fists, too, and yell the words with him. Johnny has a way of teasing them. At junior high dances, he'll leave out the four-letter word in the last chorus:

Out of control
Rampant and amok
Smokin' dope
And sayin' "——"!

And all those little teenyboppers take great pleasure in yelling it out for him. The beat gets very powerful and their little faces gleam and Johnny could take them anywhere he wants, lead them right into anarchy. I doubt that Johnny is aware of that. He enjoys the power of the moment; he laughs and thinks it's funny. It's Mike who's the political one. Anyway, the whole thing totally misses Darren's point, but it's very popular.

So, we're in the middle of rehearsal—Darren, dark and intense, playing intricate patterns on the keyboards; wiry, perpetual-motion Mike, with the mohawk and the ripped Sid Vicious Lives T-shirt, on drums; Tom, obese and sweet-faced, leaning into his bass; and me, Jessica, hunched over the guitar and frowning at the chords Darren has written out for me. I hope I don't look too uptight when I'm playing; I put the green streaks in my hair for a look-at-me devil-may-care feeling (green hair is still unusual in superprep North Bay). Johnny isn't here yet. Johnny drops into rehearsal erratically.

I was curious about Johnny long before I ever met him. The guys used to talk about him and everything he did sounded bigger than life. Other guys had girlfriends; Johnny seemed to have a harem. They call him Studly Americana, half-mocking and half-jealous. Other guys have fender benders; Johnny's accidents are dramatic, with cars flipping over and somersaulting. I like to listen to Johnny stories. I heard about his cars, his motorcycle and the two boats, the trick water skis, the Jacuzzi and the parties at his pool last summer. I missed all of those parties; that was before I joined Out of Control. I'm looking forward to this summer, though.

Johnny doesn't go to North Bay High with the rest of us. He's a senior at Bartholomew's and I wonder about that. Bartholomew's is supposed to be for dumb, rich kids who can't make it through regular high school and Johnny doesn't seem dumb. He was best friends with Tom way back in elementary school and he still hangs out with the Out of Control crowd most of the time. I guess Darren lets him get away with missing so many rehearsals because when he does show up, he's good. It's not that his voice is so great, but he puts on a terrific show. And he owns the van that transports our equipment to gigs. He's not amazingly good-looking or anything, but when Out of Control plays school dances and parties, the girls love him. Some of the stories about Johnny get bizarre and I wonder about how much is actually true. I've been in Out of Control for a month now. At first, they didn't talk that much in front of me, but now they're used to having a girl in the band and I feel like one of the guys.

I like that feeling and I hope Out of Control doesn't break up. Darren, Tom, and Johnny are all seniors; they're graduating in June. Tom's been admitted to Bard. Mike and I are juniors, so we'll still be around. I wonder what's going to happen after the summer. Darren always seems to come up with a new angle, so maybe something great will happen for Out of Control and we'll all stay together.

Darren gets up and stretches and that means we're taking a break. Finally.

"It would be nice if Studly showed up," Darren says.

"Hey, I heard he did it again," Mike says.

"Yeah, a couple of nights ago," Tom says. "He totaled the Corvette."

Darren shakes his head and Mike gives a ta-boom on the drums and laughs. "What did he do this time?"

"He drove into a wall." Tom strikes a match and it flares against the end of his cigarette. "You know that brick wall where North Road ends, right by the beach? He totaled the car and walked away without a scratch." Tom is laughing, too.

"That's not funny," I say. "He could have killed himself."

"Lighten up, Jess," Tom says. "He didn't."

"Isn't that like the third time?" I say. "My God!"

"Johnny does everything to excess. He's an excessive person." That's Mike talking and I look at him. It strikes me funny, coming from Mike with the outrageous haircut and the tattered jeans held together by safety pins, topped with one huge pin stuck through his earlobe. I start to laugh, though I think Mike's weirdness is mostly surface for shock value. He's in my social studies class, he's smart, he does his homework and normal things like that, though he's always disrupting the class and arguing with the teacher. And then I think of Johnny, who dresses so Ralph Lauren and looks like he just stepped out of the North Bay Yacht Club—and I wonder.

"What's wrong with him, anyway?" I say.

"Johnny? Nothing. Johnny's all right," Tom says.

"I can't figure him out," I say. He hasn't been around much since I've joined and I don't know him as well as the others.

"Well, watch out for him, Jessica." Mike is softly brushing the cymbals.

"No, she's not his type," Darren says. "We don't have to worry about her."

"What do you mean, I'm not his type? What's his type?"

"Beautiful and buxom," Darren says, "so you're safe, babe."

"Oh wow, that's real sparkling wit," I say, and Darren gives me his you-can't-win-them-all shrug.

If it had come from Mike or Tom, I might have smiled. Coming from Darren, it grates. And I don't like being called "babe," either.

The truth is there are days when anything from Darren grates on me. It's no big secret that Darren didn't want me in the band in the first place. He wanted Gary Vernon on guitar, but Tom and Mike both totally hate Gary, so I was a compromise.

I know Tom pushed for me. We'd been friendly around school—I think he might have had a bit of a crush on me once, but I could never think of him that way; he's truly obese. He's a great guy and we became really good friends, maybe because the boy-girl stuff was out of the way. It's a lot easier to be open with someone who doesn't expect anything from me.

Anyway, Tom was the one who told me to call Darren for an audition. Audition! It's only a high school band, for God's sake, and anybody else would have just asked to hear me play. It takes a Godlike creature like Darren to say, in that arrogant tone he gets, "All right, you can audition for me." I would have hung up right there, except that I wanted to be in this band so badly.

Actually, the first thing Darren said to me on the phone was, "What are you, a girl?"

"No, I'm a eunuch," I had answered, and we went downhill from there.

Darren gives me a look every time I make even a little mistake. I'm sure he's thinking all the time that Gary Vernon is better than me. Sometimes he makes me very nervous and I'm glad we're taking a break.

I get up from the stool I've been sitting on. My black jeans are very tight and when I sit for such a long time, they start slicing me in half. From now on, I'm going to wear sweats to rehearsal.

I'll bet he wants to do "Queen of Burger King" next. I practiced it for a long time last night and I still can't make the changes fast enough. I hope this break is a long one.

Jessica looks mad. I was kidding, but I guess she thinks I'm being obnoxious again.

I like Jessica, but I'd like her a lot better if she was in somebody else's band. She's not bad and she has good rapport with the other guys, so that's something—but I need for everyone in this group to be *great*. Especially the guitarist! She's okay as long as she's playing note by note. I have to write every single solo out for her. She can't improvise worth a damn.

I'm the only one that gives a shit, anyway. They think this is fun and games. I know how we should sound, I hear it in my head all the time, and we're almost getting it but not quite. And then Mike says rehearsal's running too long and Tom says I'm too impatient and Johnny doesn't show at all.

Johnny. If I had his kind of money, I could play piano the rest of my life and not worry about a thing. But time's running out on me.

How did it start? I was a little kid fooling around with the beat-up piano in the living room, using the low notes for thunder and the high ones for lightning, and then I picked out a tune or two. (What was the piano doing there, did it come with the house or did we inherit it or what?) I remember playing the piano when the relatives were over and everyone applauding and Mom and Dad beaming—that's when Dad was still alive—so then came the lessons and playing in the assemblies in elementary school. The teachers treated me like I was special. "First the chorus will sing 'Rudolph the Red-Nosed Reindeer' and then Darren will play a medley of . . ." In junior high, there was a stage band and I came into my own. I got all the solos. Tom, too. That's where I met Tom, Tom on bass and me on keyboards, we were the star attractions. Everyone in the whole damn school knew who I was, even the big kids. First year high school, I made all-county. That was a big deal; they announced it over the PA. That was the year Dad died. Mom got all dressed up for the concert and took George and Frankie, and I felt good that I could do something to make her look happy again.

Then I made all-state jazz ensemble and they gave me a huge solo up in Albany. Man, that was the big time, all right, playing in the well of the Legislative Building and watching the politicians staggering back from lunch. There was an article about me in the *North Bay News* (I was the only kid from North Bay that ever got an all-state *solo*) and the high school covered the bus fare. Someplace, I've got a photo of myself with State Senator Mason. And now it's all over and it don't mean shit.

It's taken me awhile, but it's finally dawned on me. All of it is to make the music departments look good. All-county. All-state. All public relations. The funny thing is, it's Mom that can't give up the dream.

Mom's face would shine when they announced my name or crowded around to congratulate me after a performance. Frankie is running wild and George is growing up too quiet and withdrawn. I'm the only one that had the chance to grow up when Dad was alive, when things were still normal: summer nights before it got dark, me and Dad tossing a baseball back and forth, the rhythm of it and the easy laughter. He was always there. Now Mom can't control Frankie and when kids pick on George, she doesn't know what to do, she can't handle it the way Dad could have. (I really loved him, my love all mixed up with the smell of tobacco and new-mown grass. But what kind of man doesn't leave any insurance or savings? What kind of man is that?) Mom needs something to be proud of so badly and I'm her daydream, her last bright hope.

I started working on a new song the other day, thinking about that.

I'm only a puppet
Populating your dream
You're pulling the strings

But I'm not what I seem
It's your own illusion
Making you cream
'Cause I'm not what I seem
No, I'm not what you need
Oh, lady
No, I'm not what you need. . . .

Songs start that way sometimes, and then turn into something else entirely by the time I've finished. The bridge isn't right yet. This one is going to wind up a boy-girl breakup and I can see Johnny punching every line. That thing about a puppet doesn't apply to Mom, anyway. All she did was give me a lot of encouragement. I was pulling my own strings. I grooved on that small-town celebrity at least as much as she did. It's just that she can't face giving it all up and I'm going to have to.

"Darren," she says, "you're so talented. You were the best in the whole state! Darren, everyone says you're so good, honey."

"There's a piano solo in all-state every year," I tell her. "Every damn year. You can lay your all-state players end-to-end and they'd reach to L.A. And the best ones, the real musicians, aren't even in all-state 'cause they're too busy getting gigs."

"But Darren, if you get into a conservatory . . ." She works so damn hard, she stuffs envelopes on the side and she still can't get it together to get the car fixed. And she's daydreaming about me in a conservatory, in the spotlight, white tie and tails.

"Dammit, Mom, I don't—"

"Please don't keep cursing like that, Darren."

"I don't want to talk about it anymore. I don't want to talk about it."

"Darren, you could try for a scholarship and then—"

"Yeah, sure. All those schools give great training to all those piano players that can't get any work except maybe training more piano players that can't get any work except for training more piano players. . . . And hey, Mom, I play rock, that's my best shot, playing rock and writing songs. . . ." And I'm going no place fast. And I can't stand to be poor anymore.

Funny, poor to Johnny means not being able to get another fifteen thousand dollar car right away and poor to Jessica means her lawn looking weedy because they can't afford lawn service and poor to me is Mom walking a mile to work to save on gas money. Dammit, I'm never going to live like that! I'll get financial aid from some SUNY school and major in something safe. I hear computers are good.

I wonder what it would feel like not to have to practice anymore.

So this summer is the end of the line—unless, maybe. There's always a maybe. The truth is that Out of Control sounds a hell of a lot better than some of the groups on MTV. So, maybe, with a little bit of luck . . . I know a guy who thinks he can set it up for an A&R man from Columbia to hear us. And then I know somebody who knows this singer that's looking for a backup band and she's cut some records. . . . We've got a gig at Three Deuces. . . . And I have a demo of us doing "Out of Control," so maybe . . .

Too much of me is tied up with playing the keyboards. Last year, I had this freak accident. I was wrestling with

Mike, just kidding around, right by the front steps of the school, and Mike twisted my finger back too far and broke it. It was the little finger on the right hand. I went to North Shore Emergency and I had to get a cast and I felt like a cripple without the piano. I felt like a cripple for that whole six weeks until I could start playing again. I'm so damn protective of my hands now. I can't fool around like that anymore. Maybe if I give the whole thing up, I can be like a normal person, even play ball without worrying about a baseball finger. I can be mediocre, a happy nothing special, just like everybody else.

Shit, I'm going to try to get this group together! I don't know what to do with Jessica. I know she's trying. The green hair is her way of trying to be part of the show, but it doesn't make it.

She's a great-looking chick, though, almost beautiful. Maybe if she wore something low-cut, danced around in front of the band, added a little sex. . . . The trouble with Jessica is that she shrinks in the spotlight. Maybe I could work with her. . . .

"Hey, Jessica?" I say.

"What?" Her face gets tight and defensive.

"Could you come over here, like Monday afternoon?"

"Monday afternoon?" Mike groans. "What, another rehearsal?"

"No, just Jessica. I have an idea I want to work out."

"Okay. Sure," Jessica says. "Sure. I'll be here right after school."

"Great. Thanks, Jess."

She looks so relieved about my not saying anything critical. It makes me feel rotten. What the hell do I think I can do, turn this chick into Tina Turner?

Oh shit, did I just tell her Monday? Yeah. Well, so be it, the sooner the better. I was supposed to do something with Barbara and I'm going to have to try to explain again. Barb's always bitching about the band coming first. That's the way it is. It does. What did she call me the other day—an emotional zombie! The band's the only thing we ever fight about and I wish she'd ease off on that.

Well, Barb's gonna kill me for this one, but I've got to do something about Jessica soon. If she could move around more, smile, *do* something. . . . We could use another crowd pleaser like Johnny. He expands in the spotlight.

Johnny's a crazy dude, but he's okay. He doesn't hit you over the head with all that wealth. He's out to have a good time and he throws it around for everyone else to enjoy, too, and you can't help liking a guy like that. And if he drinks himself unconscious, well, that's Johnny. When Johnny has an escapade, it's funny. If it was me, I'd be a bum. What gets me is he's so damn good and he can't read a note of music. And I wish to hell he'd show up.

Jessica

Darren sounded pretty pleasant. He's probably going to help me with something Monday afternoon. Or even give me more stuff to do. . . . No, I doubt that.

It's not that I can't play the guitar. I took classical lessons for a few years and I was good, but this is different. Finger picking and reading notes and the soft reverberation of an acoustic guitar on a Renaissance piece—it was so well-ordered and quiet and carefully measured. Too quiet to be noticed. I think I needed to cut loose on an electric. Darren's music isn't simple and I haven't been using a pick for that long. I've got to practice more. I like being in this band and I don't want to mess up.

It's something like being on a team. My brother Larry was a jock and before he went away to college, guys from his teams would always be around our house. I envied that whole feeling about them. I mean, I had friends, but they had something extra, more than friendship. It was that team feeling, that camaraderie, all for one, and when the ice hockey team got into the play-offs, there was all that excitement and togetherness.

I ran track for a while in junior high, but then I started smoking. Track was a more individual thing, anyway. I was also on the Mathletes, which sounds like a joke. I love math. I love the precision of it and knowing there can only be one right answer. I love the uncomplicated neatness of it. Tom says I like math because I'm afraid to take chances, that I always need to play it safe. (I green-streaked my hair though, didn't I?) Anyway, the Mathletes didn't exactly have that jock feeling.

I didn't expect to miss Larry so much when he left for college. It was better when Larry was home, keeping things stirred up and getting everyone's attention. He left a vacuum. Now it's just Mom and Dad, mainly ignoring each other, and everyone going off into their own corners: Mom, lost in a book, Dad watching TV, and me in my room with the door shut tight. Sometimes I turn the volume way up when I'm practicing until the house shakes and rattles.

Being in Out of Control has that team feeling. On the way to a gig, crowded into the van along with all the equipment, we feel so close and tight, even Darren and me. It's like us against the civilians. It's like belonging to a special kind of family. I really like hanging out with that whole Out of Control crowd. Being in the band puts me on the inside. Their girlfriends come and go. I have a special position at the nucleus.

I'm proud of being part of a band that's so outstanding. Something good has to happen for us. Darren's immensely talented. He writes all the songs and everyone says they're amazing. (Mike's favorites are anything about lobotomies—he'd like us to get more into hardcore.) I like the new one, "Bag Lady Blues," so much. You think it's about a shopping bag lady, pathetic, hunting through garbage cans, and then, with the slightest twist, it turns out to be about one of those North Shore princesses, with shopping bags from Fiorucci's and Gucci, spending a lifetime going through the stores and somehow equally pathetic. The melody is haunting. You can examine Darren's songs like a cut jewel, turning them this way and that to catch different lights.

When I'm feeling mellow, I think that if Darren comes on arrogant, maybe he's got the right.

"Okay," Darren is saying, " 'Queen of Burger King.' Let's do it."

I sigh and put my earplugs back in—Dad says I have to wear them so I won't go deaf and I think that it's cute that he gets protective like that, in spurts. We go into "Queen." We do it twice. I am concentrating so hard that

I don't notice anyone coming in. When I look up, I see Johnny sitting on the orange crate in the corner with Ray and Barbara. Johnny is pale and thin, with black hair, longish and feathered back. His arm is bandaged and he looks especially pale tonight, almost green in this light.

I catch his eye and smile. My smile is my best feature because I have good teeth and very deep dimples. He's looking at me intensely, unsmiling. My eyes are locked into his and I screw up the next chord.

"Knock off, kiddies!" Barbara calls out. "Time's up, it's five past nine."

At nine o'clock, we turn into pumpkins. Darren lives in the part of North Bay where the houses are small and very close together. There is a thin strip of grass separating his house from the one next door. There's been a running battle with the neighbors about our noise and their baby not getting to sleep. It was pretty hairy for a while. Darren's mother got into it and worked out a truce. We have to quit playing promptly at nine until we get more soundproofing. We've been careful about it, but we get dirty looks all the time. Now the neighbors on the other side have started complaining about the traffic, because kids drop by after rehearsal and it turns into parties. They're complaining that somebody's always blocking their driveway, but that only happened twice. I think his rotten neighbors are what inspired Darren's "Out of Control" lyrics.

Darren's basement is still the best place, though. It gets damp down here and it floods when it rains, so there's always this funny smell, but it has a separate entrance, so we can all come and go and leave our stuff without going through the house. And, most important, Darren's mother doesn't mind our being here. She even likes us. Once, she cooked up a big pot of spaghetti and brought it down to us. I wish my mom were more like her.

"Come on, nine o'clock!" That's Barbara again. She's got a lot of patience; she spends a lot of time waiting around for Darren to get through.

Darren is unplugging the amplifier and rolling up the cord. I go across the room for my guitar case. It's against the wall near Johnny.

"Hi," I say.

"Hi. It sounds good."

"Darren doesn't think so," I say. "Especially me."

"Don't worry about Darren. He's some kind of friggin' perfectionist."

"No, it's me. The guitar part of 'Queen' is murder." I'm snapping the locks on the case. "I've been practicing, but I have all that other stuff to learn, too."

He's listening to me like he's really curious about what I'm saying and wants to catch every word. I think a lot of his charm is in that look of great interest. All I'm doing is complaining, so I stop talking.

"Yo, Johnny!" Darren calls from across the room. "Good of you to stop by!"

"Don't hassle me, man! I'm getting all the grief I need at home, okay? I had to ride over with Ray and Barbara, they won't give me a damn car to drive now, not even the van!"

"I heard about the car," I say. "How are you, anyway? What happened to your arm?"

"It's okay," he says. "Some glass splinters got in it, that's all. It's okay."

"I'm glad you're all right. You were so lucky!"

"Yeah, I know. The whole front got mashed in." He's half laughing. "You should see it, it looks like an accordion."

"What happened?"

"I can't remember too much about it and that's the truth." The basement light is making green shadows under his cheekbones. "I don't remember driving into any wall. I was leaving Three Deuces. Joe Bourne was tending bar and I was kidding around with him. That's the last thing I remember."

He looks confused.

"That must be an awful feeling," I say, finally.

"I was just a little buzzed, that's all."

I don't know what to say to that.

"I got to change the whole scene, that's the problem. Darren's basement, Three Deuces, Darren's basement. It gets boring. Look at it. Look around you. It's the same people doing the same things all the time."

A bunch of kids have come in, carrying six-packs. Barbara is talking to Darren, her lips in a thin, angry line. Mike is passing a joint around and there are some girls giggling up at him. Darren's little brother Frankie, who is bad news, has sneaked downstairs and is trying to cop a beer. The stereo is turned down so you can hardly hear the music, but the beat-beat-beat comes through. There is a hubbub of noise all around us and Johnny and I are alone in a little circle of quiet.

"I guess I see what you mean," I say uncertainly.

"No. You haven't been hanging out with us that long. I oughta change my life around. . . ." He laughs but I think I see shadows around his eyes. "What the hell, it'll pass."

I don't know what to say. Mike calls him over and then I'm talking to Tom and my friend Annie. The crowd swallows us up and we never do connect again that night.

At one point, I glance over at Johnny through the crush in the basement and there is this blond woman hanging on to his good arm. I say woman, because she's not in high school, that's for sure. Her hair is up in a French twist and she's wearing dark red lipstick. There's lots of cleavage and she looks in her twenties. He's smiling, but he looks tired and I'm sure the bandaged arm is aching. She is looking up at him with an adoring expression, a kind of rapt "Oh, Johnny!" look. I'm really surprised. I mean, this older, good-looking blond woman hanging on to a skinny eighteen-year-old's arm!

Tom watches me watching and says, "Studly Americana rides again."

Jessica

*I*t is Sunday morning and I am sitting at the dining room table, drinking coffee and eating pancakes. Mom and Dad are eating, too. Usually, we have breakfast separately; everyone makes their own toast or whatever, but this time, Mom made pancakes and it's the kind of thing you have to serve to three people at once.

Dad is reading the *New York Times* and not looking

at the fork that goes back and forth between his plate and his mouth. He is reading out loud now, something about the Dow Jones and the prime rate. Mom's eyes are glazed. Once in a while, she fills in a pause with "Mmm-hmm." That's the extent of their conversations.

This is the warmest day we've had so far. I see the sun shining outside the dining room and it looks inviting. It looks like it might be the first beach day. The dining room, though, is plunged into gloom because of the huge wild cherry tree that grows directly in front of the window. Mom wanted to have it cut down for the longest time and Dad kept saying we can't afford a tree service and he can't do it himself. Nothing has been said about it recently. It's been there for the twelve years we've lived in this house and it keeps growing. In the summer, the cherries fall on the front walk and we have lots of fun slipping on the pits.

Our house is a large southern colonial, with those columns in front. We're in a good neighborhood—half-acre zoning, trees, nice landscaping. It's not fantastic like Ocean Point, where Johnny lives, but it's nice. The trouble is they can't afford to keep it up. I keep hearing about taxes getting higher and the recession and Dad's business going downhill. Things they can't afford to fix are falling apart all around us. The dishwasher stopped working awhile ago. What makes Mom most grim, though, are the things crumbling outside that everyone can see. I wish they'd just move to a small house in some inexpensive neighborhood. I couldn't care less. I guess those southern columns are a status symbol to her; maybe she thinks she's living in Tara.

I watch the butter melt in the center of my pancake.

Mom does make great pancakes, with cinnamon and vanilla flavoring. I spread the puddle of maple syrup with the side of my fork and watch it leave a sticky trail.

There's a long silence and they have nothing to say to each other, so eventually they'll pick on me. Then they can be united.

"Jessica," Mom says, "I wish you would consider doing something about your hair."

"Like what?"

"You know what I mean! Just because you put those awful streaks in doesn't mean they can't be dyed over. . . ."

"Green hair!" Dad says.

"It's terrible, Jessica! It's unladylike and it's—"

"It's only hair, Mom, and it's mine!"

I feel the knot in my stomach start to form. I don't know exactly why I did it. It seemed like a cool idea at the time—old news in New York, but different for North Bay. I'm not a drug addict, I don't drink much and never in a closet, I'm probably the only sixteen-year-old virgin left in the Western Hemisphere, and they're going to crucify me because of six green streaks?

They're going on and on. Should I sing "It's Not Easy Being Green"? No, I'd better not. That would prolong it. Do kids still watch "Sesame Street"? That seems so long ago. . . . Were we more of a family then, or was I too young to notice?

". . . and a hairdresser could cover it over and . . ."

If Larry were here, they could have a sparkling conversation about North Bay's last game instead. God, Mom was proud of Larry! His marks weren't that hot, but he got a scholarship to Colgate on the strength of being the fastest slapshot in the East. Larry, the family star. I miss him, anyway.

". . . your crowning glory . . . stubborn and self-destructive . . ."

Glorious Gloria. Mom has wonderful thick hair. It's golden brown and curly. She knows it's wonderful, so she wears it longer than someone past the big four-oh should. Her face is a letdown next to all that great hair. She looks disappointed and puffy. She looks pretty good with makeup, but she never bothers anymore when it's just for Dad.

Sometimes I wonder if all marriages are like this close up. Maybe all families are dead when they're by themselves and not putting up a front. How am I supposed to know? We're very charming to each other in public. Well, basic instinct tells me there's got to be something better.

". . . and maybe it's the influence of that group you go around with. That sullen Damian . . . he lives near the bridge, doesn't he?"

"Darren," I say.

". . . and the weird one . . ."

"Mike?"

"I don't *know* those boys, but—"

"You know Tom."

"Well, I know his parents and at least he's from a good family, but he *is* grotesque, Jessica, and I'd think a pretty girl could find nicer . . . Larry's friends were just a different *kind*!"

"I'm not a cheerleader, Mom. I don't want to be a cheerleader. You didn't like the Mathletes, either. You said they were nerds."

"If you would listen to me, Jessie," Mom is saying.

I don't want to listen. I don't want to be anything like her. I tune out. I mean, look how she wound up.

"Gloria, pass the syrup," Dad says.

No one really hears anyone else in this house, anyway. I fill my mouth with pancake. I think about the way Johnny listens, looking intensely interested. I think I like Johnny. But I picture Johnny's life as a French farce, with bedroom doors and closet doors opening and slamming shut, hiding half-nude ladies. I'm not his type.

I lick some maple syrup off my fork. Then I escape to call Tom and see if anyone is going to the beach.

Johnny

I took the van. I can't make it without wheels. We get to Jones Beach in two carloads. Darren, Barbara, and Jessica are in Mike's car. I've got Tom, Annie, Dale, and everybody else. We go to Field 2. You meet everybody from North Bay High on Field 2. Don't know how that got started, but it's been like that every summer. Only today, it's too windy—whose bright idea was this, anyhow?—and there are hardly any other people. The wire garbage cans are almost empty and it's us and a crowd of seagulls.

"I thought you couldn't get the van anymore," Tom says.

"They changed their minds. Consistency isn't their big feature."

I don't want to think about the Corvette. I had it fixed

up with all this stuff—a fuzz buster, a special horn that played "This Bud's for You," a tape deck—and I had louvers for the rear window on order. They're supposed to come next week. There wasn't a scratch on it, either, because I was careful not to go where the branches could scratch at it. It looked new as it was three months ago. That was one beautiful little car with a spotless white finish. What did I go and mess up like that for? Thinking about that car makes me sick to my stomach.

Everyone's towels are blowing on the sand. Jessica's spreading a bright blue beach towel and anchoring the corners with sneakers. She's got her own Nikes and she just stole someone else's pair for the other two corners. It's cute the way she's so neat about everything.

"How's the arm, Johnny?" she goes.

"It's okay. The bandage is for sympathy, so you'll be nice to me."

I like her quick smile.

"Hey, Jessica," I say, "did anyone ever drown in those dimples?"

I watch her peeling off her sweatshirt. She's wearing a light pink bikini and her skin is still too untanned against it. Her skin is the color of the inside of a banana. She's got nice long legs. I sit down on the edge of her towel and she shifts over a little. She smells like coconut oil. Coconut, banana—I must be hungry for fruit salad.

Some of the kids start tossing a Frisbee.

Mike has a joint and offers a toke and it makes me kind of sad to shake my head no.

Smoking grass on the beach was always one of my nicest things. I mean, like all last summer. On a clear, bright day, I could get into the sun's rays shimmering on the water and all the individual little grains of sand. The reason I don't do much pot anymore is because of this experience I had. I'd still like to know what it was, if it was laced with something or what. I'd been getting a little paranoid before that, anyway, but that particular night, we were all hanging out at the golf course, a whole gang of us, sitting around and talking and like that. All of a sudden, the sound of the crickets got louder and louder. It got so loud that it was blotting out everything else. People's lips were moving with no sound coming out. I didn't want anyone to know, so I moved over and sat by myself and clapped my hands over my ears. The cricket sound was so loud, it was hurting. All I wanted to do was get home, but, like in some weird dream, it was like I wasn't allowed to leave unless I had a good excuse to give everybody. Trying to think of a reason to get away and the noise not letting me think. So I'm sitting off to the side with the sound at overpowering volume and then I can't see. Nothing. I'm blind. It might have been fifteen minutes, half an hour, two hours, I don't know. Pitch black. After awhile, the noise went down and my eyesight came back. Nobody noticed and I just went on home. But that was some bad scene, man.

I took to it at first, so I'd light up before school and during school and after school. But after awhile, I couldn't even remember what I had for dinner the night before and then, after that cricket-blind scene, I just about quit. If it stops being fun, what's the point? I was never a real burnout. Anyway, there's a lot of other stuff.

That happens to me a lot, though, things starting off good and then turning sour. Tom and I were talking about that the other night. He said I go overboard on everything.

Tom was talking about the accident and my drinking. It's just because I get bored and drinking relaxes me. So I'll throw down the tequila sunrises when everybody else is playing quarters with beers. I don't *have* to, though. Just as long as there's something that makes me feel good. I always want more of a good thing, that's all. Same with sex. When I first got into sex, man, I couldn't get enough. After awhile, arms, legs, faces, names become interchangeable. Ludes help; they make it last longer and mean more. I don't know. Maybe I'm ready for something else.

My mouth feels like cotton and I'm getting a headache. I get up and go down to the water.

It's too cold for the beach, I'm thinking too much, I feel like shit and coming here was a dumb idea.

The sand is cold where the tide's been. I start to walk down a way. I'm walking along slowly, by myself, kind of thinking about everything, and you know that feeling you get when something's behind you? That kind of crawly feeling? Well, I turn around real fast and it's Jessica, laughing. She's walking right behind me, single file.

"What are you doing?" I say.

"Walking in your footsteps," she says, laughing. I see her take a big step to get her foot in the right place and she's caught up to me. "Come on, jog with me."

"No, I don't feel like it."

I go on walking and she's right behind me again, following my trail like some little kid playing a game. Crazy broad! I look at her over my shoulder and she's got this cute, teasing smile.

"Oh, come on, Johnny. I don't want to run by myself."

"So don't run."

"Oh, come on," she goes. "Come on. You'll warm up. Come on. It's good for you. Come on, Johnny." All through this, she's jumping into my footprints.

She's different, that's for sure. She's some kind of original.

She's making me smile. "Hey, crazy broad, get away from me!" I start jogging away from her and she's right behind me. In a little while, she's right alongside and going fast and I'm working to keep up with her.

We're running on the edge of the sand, where the water's pulling back and forth, and it splashes with each step. If I look down at the water moving under me, I get dizzy. It's ice cold on my feet.

I go along like that for a while, not talking, busy breathing, and then I slow to a stop. She keeps going and I watch her. She's got great form. Some girls flop all over the place when they run. I like the way the muscles in her legs work, that healthy, high-energy, charged-up look about her. I ought to get healthier. She goes a way and then turns and doubles back to me. She's panting a little now, no makeup, shiny from the coconut suntan gloop, just beginning to get some color, all peachy and pink.

"Wasn't that good?" she gasps.

"No."

"Don't you ever run?"

"No. What for?"

"Well, the way you would do a sport," she says.
"Running to no place is boring. I ski, I swim, I—"
"Okay. Let's go swimming."
The ocean is as rough as I've seen it, great waves, great for surfing. We push each other in and my body turns numb. It's freezing! We jump the waves for a while and we get into this sand fight, throwing handfuls of wet sand and trying to get each other's hair. She's coming at me with this big handful and we're wrestling and I say, "Hey! Watch the arm!" She stops short, right away, looking sorry. So I get her and then I feel bad, because that was a phony and she fell for it. We kind of wrestle some more and I'm holding her, and that's no accident. Her body fits right into mine, pieces of a crossword puzzle that just work out. She says something but her voice gets lost in the roar. This is some rough ocean. Her lips taste bitter-salty and I kiss her for a long, long time.
The place where we left everybody is just a couple of dots of beach towel colors.
We're both freezing and we fall into a slow jog going back. "We shoulda taken our sweatshirts," I say.
I look over at her. Her face sure changes fast. All that sparkle-energy is gone, she's shivering and she has that scared little-girl look again. That's what I noticed the other night at Darren's, when the band was playing. She had that same look, the tip of her tongue out on her lips, frowning into the music. Concentrating hard, having a bad time, a little kid under that crazy hair.
"Give me your hand, Jessica."
She looks up at me fast, startled, and hesitates a moment before she gives it to me.

Just what I thought. Her nails are all chewed up.

I hold her hand the rest of the way back and I feel tender for her.

We get back and pull sweatshirts on—hers is white with North Bay Hockey in red letters—and we're still freezing. Everybody's standing around at the water's edge. Darren's gone in and he's waving for everyone else to come, but no one's moving much. Mike and Tom are in knee deep, trying to edge in an inch at a time. Mike is blown. Two cute girls in jeans walk right by him on the sand and I see his face working, groping for an opening line.

He finally comes up with, "Hi! How's the water?"

These chicks take a look at his legs in the ocean, do a double take, and keep on going fast. Tom and I collapse, laughing.

"What's the matter?" Mike goes. "What did I say?"

Tom just shakes his head, helplessly laughing, and I see his body shake like Jell-O under the T-shirt. He keeps a T-shirt on all the time, even when it's hot, even when he goes swimming. We go back a long way, back when he was the fat kid that everyone picked on in elementary school and I used to stick up for him. That's one thing about knowing somebody for a long time; it cuts right through the crap. Tom goes around wearing this black leather jacket over all the bulk and he's role-playing the tough honcho in a hot rock band. I remember him crying when they used to chant "Chubbsy-wubbsy, Chubbsy-wubbsy" at him on the school bus.

Tom remembers me from when I used to get the reading all mixed up and Mrs. Kallen, that bitch, would make me turn red the way she kept harping on it. I was just a little kid and I'd get all red in front of the whole class. I still get the letters turned around. That's dyslexia. That's why I couldn't hack it at North Bay and had to transfer to Bartholomew's. They got this special program for dyslexics, but who gives a shit? I don't need their books; I'll take the VCR anytime. I got too much style to let any of that bother me now.

What am I thinking about this stuff for? Why do I keep bringing myself down?

I look over at Jessica and she gives me this little smile. I smile back and then her face opens up, warm and sunny and the dimples a mile deep. She makes me feel so good, I almost laugh out loud. This girl could replace uppers.

Jessica

As we leave the beach, Johnny says to me, under his breath, "Get into the van."

I had planned to kind of maneuver myself into the van for the trip home, anyway, but I guess Johnny doesn't need to be subtle. I squeeze between him and Tom in the front seat and Annie gets into Mike's car in my place. She doesn't care.

"It's a toss-up anyway," she grins at me, "whether Mike's motor dies or whether Johnny crashes."

I look up at Johnny. I'm pretty sure he's sober.

When we get back to North Bay, Johnny drops everyone else off and saves me for last. He's crisscrossing any logical route to do it and I'm glad. I don't think anyone notices except for Tom. Tom gives me a funny look as he gets out.

Johnny watches the road and shifts into gear.

"Are you in any hurry to get home?" he says.

"No . . . not really."

He glances at me through thick black eyelashes and nods slightly, as if something has been settled between us.

"We'll go to my house," he says.

I have a chilled sensation and I don't know if it's fear or desire or both.

"I've got an outdoor Jacuzzi. Heated. It's great after the beach."

"Oh," I say.

"I think my stepmother's home," Johnny says.

"Oh," I say. "Okay."

What about his stepmother? Is he saying that he's not going to pounce on me? I don't know if I'm glad or sorry. I've been curious about Johnny or fascinated by his reputation or attracted to his freewheeling style for a long time. I guess I was planning something when I followed him down the beach. So this is turning out exactly the way I wanted, I think. My lips feel bruised from his kiss and that's strange, because he wasn't rough at all. Johnny kissing me and rough waves pushing and pulling at us. It was a long, long kiss and I held on, shaky, mauled by the ocean, ready to let myself drown in him.

"Why so quiet?" he says.

"I don't know. Just thinking."

Just scared. Tom, Mike, even my brother think I'm a daredevil. I'll plunge into all kinds of things—I'll schuss down a mountain, run the fastest, dive off the highest board. That's easy; I only have to trust myself. This is different. This, meaning sex—because that's what it's about, isn't it?

We're driving into the Ocean Point area. There are hidden houses at the ends of long driveways and big trees and iron gates. We pass a corral and I get a glimpse of horses through the shrubbery lining the road.

I look at his profile. Darren is, strictly speaking, better looking, but it's Johnny that I want. I've fantasized sleeping with Johnny. I've also fantasized sleeping with the Mick Jagger of those early posters with the codpiece stuffed tights. Unattainable and unthreatening. But Johnny is here, now, with his thigh against mine, and I wonder if he could even suspect that I've never seen a man in the flesh.

I like the way he moves. I like his eyes, black with long black lashes. His eyes are very dark against the white of his skin. The very fair skin is a surprise against raven black hair.

"You didn't tan at all today," I say.

"I don't tan. I burn. I had a couple pounds of sunblock on."

The skin of his neck looks sensitive and pink. "I think you missed a spot."

"Man, I've had some painful burns!" He glances over at me. "Now you. You've turned all peach and gold. I ought to get a transfusion."

He's half smiling. Transfusion? Johnny sinking his teeth into my neck, drawing blood, sucking blood. Weird images. He probably meant to use another word entirely.

He's driving fast. There's a part of Ocean Point that looks almost like an ordinary North Bay neighborhood, except for nicer houses and more space between them because of two-acre zoning. We're now in the other section where acreage loses all meaning. This is Great Gatsby country. We're reading F. Scott Fitzgerald in American lit and they say his East Egg is around here. I am imagining Johnny slouched in a white suit, crystal champagne glass in hand. Somehow it fits. He's the only one of us I can imagine that way.

"I should have taken the bandage off," he says.

"Is it uncomfortable?"

"Wet and sandy," he says.

I wonder why we're talking about tans and bandages. I'm thinking of when he's going to kiss me again and if it'll feel the same way.

We're driving on what I think is a side road and it turns out to be Johnny's driveway. It goes down to the bay. The house is all angles and triangles, made of glass and pale wood. It looks like a boat hanging over the rocky beach.

He parks the van next to a shiny black Mercedes. No sign of the wrecked Corvette. Gravel scrunches underfoot. We pass a tennis court. The pool is in back. It's large and there are rock formations all around the sides. It's empty, the bottom painted black, a deep black pit.

"It'll be ready some time next week," Johnny says.

"This is nice," I say. "I bet when it's filled, it looks like a real pond."

There are white-flowered rhododendrons all around.

"See those rocks up there?" Johnny says. "It's rigged to work like a waterfall."

"That must be beautiful."

"You'll see this summer."

"I heard about all the parties last year," I say.

"Yeah, it was a funny summer."

We are at the Jacuzzi, a miniature of the pool, also surrounded by rocks.

"How hot do you want it? About eighty?"

"Great."

He turns a knob and the water begins to churn.

We are peeling off jeans and sweatshirts. My legs are beginning to show tan and I'm glad. He reaches over and his fingertips are brushing the skin on my shoulders and back. My skin feels singed and I jump.

"There's sand all over you," he says. "You don't want to clog the drain, do you?" With his back to the sun, I can't see the pupils of his eyes.

I nod and let him continue brushing the sand. I feel the heat in my body. Maybe I got too much sun for the first day out. Maybe the day has suddenly turned tropical.

He's pulling the adhesive off his bandage, awkwardly, with one hand. I help him. I unwind the gauze, touching his skin, Johnny watching me. I touch the marks—hardened scratches that look like they'll be scars. My hand runs along his arm and then I pull it away, quickly, self-consciously.

"Does it hurt?" I say.

"A little." He's watching my face.

We ease into the Jacuzzi. A cloud of steam rises above the water. I see a flowering magnolia through the haze. The pink-and-white petals on the tree are waxy and incandescent. There are dead petals on the ground, brown with decay.

Johnny is next to me. I am very aware of the inch of space separating our bodies. He tilts his head back and closes his eyes.

The steam makes the afternoon shimmer. I see rings around the sun.

I can't relax, even in the comforting warmth. I try tilting my head back, too, resting it on the edge. The bubbles are under and over and around my body. I squint at the sky and the colors are a kaleidoscope of blue and green and yellow. Bubbles are pulsing between my fingers.

"Hey, Jessica," he says lazily, "go get us some cigarettes. In my pants pocket."

"I don't want to get out," I say. The bubbles are blurring the outlines of his legs, his blue bathing suit, the hard bulge. . . .

"Come on, don't be so lazy."

"You get them." My voice sounds breathy.

"Come on, Jessica."

"Do all your girls serve you?"

"Are you going to be like that?" He is half sitting, over me. "Are you going to give me a hard time?"

"I don't know."

I feel something sudden and sharp, a pin prick, deep inside the very bottom of my stomach. He is very close to me, shutting out the sky. "Then I guess we won't smoke," he says.

I know he's going to kiss me before he leans over. He moves maddeningly slowly and I arch up to meet him. I'm shaking with anticipation. I've been waiting ever since he brushed the sand off my shoulders. The steam wraps a blanket of fog around us and the boundaries of our bodies are washing away. This is like it was before, in the ocean, even deeper. Every part of me is tuned into him. We shift a little and fit together.

There is a faint smell of gasoline and burning charcoal. Somewhere, someone must be starting a barbecue. It is all far away. His hand is playing with my bathing suit strap and his little finger is drifting down, further down. . . . There is no other world. There is no sense of time. I am sinking. . . .

"This is better than a shower," he mutters.

What? I am jarred. What am I doing here, with Johnny of all people? I don't know what he expects of me, I can't . . .

"What's the matter, Jessica?"

It's hard to find my voice. "Listen," I say. "I don't take showers."

"Oh, yeah?" He laughs. "What do you do, use a lot of perfume?"

"You know what I mean," I say.

"No problem. Whenever you're ready," he says.

His hands are drifting over my skin, underwater to my thighs. I deliberately turn myself off.

"What's the matter?" he says. "What are you scared of?"

I'm scared of Johnny, everything I've heard about Johnny. I was curious, but . . . not now, not yet. I don't even know him. When the girls talk about being "swept away" it makes me nervous. The idea of losing myself is terrifying. . . . The last time I went out with someone, it was kid stuff. Johnny would demand more. . . .

"What's wrong, Jessica?"

We're apart and he's waiting for an answer. I reach to say something light. "I guess I've heard too many stories about your harem," I say, trying to smile.

"Don't believe everything you hear," he says. "I'm not like that. You know what happens. When you buy drinks for everyone, all the barflies start attaching themselves to you."

I remember Tom talking about Johnny buying drinks for the house someplace late one Friday night. Tom says all the bartenders in town know Johnny. And sometimes take him home.

"Tell me something," he says. "Have you ever done it?"

I look away from him miserably. I know I came on to him and I don't think Johnny is the type to play games. I can't lie now and I can't deflect a direct question. "No," I say. I'm embarrassed.

There's a long silence. I've got to break it somehow. "I'm making the *Guinness Book of World Records* next week. Last virgin in North Bay."

It's not that funny, but he laughs. "So we gotta hold out for the week? Okay, relax, I'm not gonna jump your bones."

I look up at him. It's the imperfections about his mouth that make it so sensual: the very slight overbite, the pouty lower lip.

"You know something? I haven't even had a *real* girlfriend since like ninth grade."

"Oh?"

"That's the truth. I never have enough patience to wait for anybody that I'd want for a regular girlfriend. . . ."

That fits with the Johnny I know. He cuts out of

parties as soon as things get slow. He gets restless and bored. He's an instant-gratification person. I can see that.

"I oughta get something real going in my life," he goes on.

What doesn't fit is the little glimpses of sadness I'm seeing.

"You've got your whole life ahead. There'll be lots of things—" I start to say.

"Wait, I'm okay. You're very quick with the sympathy. I noticed that about you."

"When?"

"When we had the sand fight. The second I said 'watch the arm,' you looked so sorry."

"I thought I'd really hurt you."

"You know how rotten I felt? I'm sorry I took advantage. You made me feel so rotten."

I start laughing. "Did you really feel bad? Did you really?"

"Yeah. What's so funny?"

"If I'd had a bandage, I would've done exactly the same thing. My older brother's faster and stronger, so I did things like that all the time to get an even chance."

"You mean you're a very rotten person, too?"

"I guess so."

He's looking at me so hard. My voice trails off and we're left looking into each other's eyes. Our bodies flow together again. We sink back into the water. It's warm and urgent and I have the delicious feeling he's as attracted to me as I am to him.

Later, we go into the house and I meet his stepmother, Laurel. She's sitting in the living room, doing nothing.

She has the vague, bewildered look of someone who should be wearing glasses, but isn't. She's very pretty and too young to be someone's mother. She's wearing a long white caftan with blue embroidery. I mumble through the introductions because I know I look messy. My lips feel puffy and my bathing suit is making damp patches through my jeans.

We go through the hall and up the stairs. They don't have risers; they are floating, suspended in space. There are huge, oddly shaped plants throwing shadows on walls covered with rough white silk. Everything looks expensive and I can't help being impressed.

I follow him into his room and I look around. Two pale gray lacquered armoires connected by a light bridge over a water bed. Stereo and CDs—at a glance, I see Springsteen and Sting. A rack with guns. A Kawasaki motorcycle poster.

"Your stepmother's very pretty. She looks like a model."

"She used to be a cocktail waitress. That was before they got married. Now she takes care of the baby."

"The baby?"

"Yeah. I got a two-year-old half brother. Laurel's okay. She's a little spacey, but we get along okay. She does her thing and I do mine."

I wonder how the two-year-old manages those floating stairs. There is no sign of him.

"Is your real mother—"

"Dead? No, she's in Florida."

I pick up a metal figurine. "What's this?"

"Fourth grade soccer trophy. I was a little jock up to seventh grade."

Johnny played soccer, I file away. I am fascinated with every bit of information.

"Am I asking too many questions?"

He laughs. "No."

I want to know everything about him and I can see he likes that. I touch his things.

"A water bed?"

"I have insomnia. A water bed's supposed to float me to sleep."

"Does it?"

"No, but they'll buy me anything to keep me calmed down."

"Do you have insomnia all the time?"

"I don't know. I used to do a lot of speed and that messed up my sleep pattern. Sometimes I have nightmares and sometimes I can't get to sleep. It might have started with the speed, I don't remember."

"Oh."

"I don't do it anymore."

"It's supposed to be so terrible for you."

"I was jumping all the time. I lost fifteen pounds. No, I'm down to just a little nose candy for my birthday and for Christmas."

It sounds like he's straightened out. The guns are on a rack near his bed. I hope he doesn't hunt.

He sees me looking. "Don't worry, they're not loaded now."

"No, it's not that. I was wondering if you hunt." I almost hold my breath for his answer.

"No. I do some target shooting."

"Oh." I am so relieved. I didn't want anything to spoil how much I like him.

". . . and I load them when I'm alone in the house, like at night. We've been ripped off and they broke in through my window. No one was home that time, but—"

"I'm so glad you don't hunt! You know Mike's T-shirt, the I Shot Bambi one? I know it's just for shock, but it still makes me feel awful."

"Yeah? I never did get that."

"Well, you know, *Bambi*. Remember that scene where the hunters kill his mother? I cried and cried."

"I never saw it."

"You never saw *Bambi*? Well, you read it, didn't you, or maybe—?"

"No, I don't know about it. I've heard the name, though."

"But everyone . . . every kid . . . ," I say. Didn't anyone read bedtime stories to him or take him to Disney movies? I can't imagine what kind of a child he was. "Did you have a teddy bear?"

"Did I have a what?"

"A teddy bear or something to sleep with? I had a Winnie the Pooh."

He's laughing at me. "No, nothing like that. I need a Jessica to sleep with. To see me through the night."

He's kidding, I know, but there's that unexpected bit of vulnerability coming through. Like when he was talking about being alone in the house with the gun. And he seemed so uncomfortable when I asked him about reading *Bambi*. He's not as confident as I expected. There's something little-boy-lost about him. That's why I reach out and take his hand. He holds mine and doesn't let go.

Later, when he asks me to go out, I'm really happy.

I'm not that surprised and I don't even feel that much beyond my depth anymore. I don't know exactly what I'm getting into, but I like him and I'm not going to back off.

Mike

Monday morning, 10:30. I'm supposed to go over next semester's schedule with Mrs. Coyle, my guidance counselor. No sweat; I've fulfilled just about all the boring requirements, so senior year should be a gas. Anyway, I like her.

She's looking through my file on her desk.

"Michael," she says, "your PSATs were extremely high. High enough to be in the running for a Merit Scholarship."

Her big brown eyes are earnestly searching mine. She's great looking, for an older chick. I'm a sucker for big brown eyes. Listen, I'm not gonna discriminate on account of age. . . .

"The classes you want to take next year aren't too challenging. I think you should reconsider—"

"Mrs. Coyle," I say, "Music Theory is one of the toughest courses in the school, at least the way Giacomo teaches it."

"Maybe, but the colleges will be looking for more *academic*—you want Advanced Wood Shop, Acting I—?"

"And Advanced Placement History," I say.

"That's good, but—"

"I like carving wood. What makes abstractions so much better than craftsmanship?"

She sighs. "Where are you thinking of applying?"

"I don't know for sure. I was thinking, maybe Stanford?" I read in the *Times* the other day about the Incomparable Stanford Marching Band being reprimanded for arriving at football games drunk and spelling out obscenities. They don't wear uniforms or march, and they have a rock and roll repertoire. *And* they present political satires at halftime, which gets them in all kinds of trouble. Definitely my kind of people and a nice switch from the squeaky-clean California image . . .

"Stanford might be a bit of a reach—your grades are uneven. But your GPA isn't bad, and with outstanding SATs and challenging senior courses . . . Wherever you decide to apply, a personal interview could help; you're very articulate and you can be rather charming and—uh—I'm assuming you'd modify your look?"

"You're actually asking me to change my persona?" I say, outraged.

She smiles. "Those safety pins look dangerous," she says. "I hope you're careful."

"I've had my tetanus shot."

"Why the hair, Michael?"

"What's wrong with it? The Mohawks," I say, "had a lot of sense. The Indians knew no one could own the earth any more than the moon or stars; they used the land and passed it on for future—"

"Okay, all right." I'm putting her on and she knows it. "You'll have to decide whether to compromise yourself just long enough to get through an interview. At least we don't have to worry about that until next year."

I've had my hair so many different ways, I don't know what I look like. "I don't know what I'll be next year."

"Older, I think," she says. She hands me a sheet of paper. "Please fill out a new list of extracurricular activities for me; I'll need it for your recommendations. 'Shark hunting, keelhauling.' That's a little sophomoric for you, isn't it?"

"True," I admit.

"You're very bright and persuasive. If you were more positive, you could be a leader."

"There's no place worth leading to. And when everything's rotten to the core, the only thing left is to say no."

She shakes her pretty head. "I'd love to see you using all that energy *for* something."

"Can I ask you something, Mrs. Coyle? What were you doing at my age?"

"What was I doing?" She glances at her watch.

"Were you in the Woodstock generation? Were you active or uninvolved?"

"I suppose somewhat involved. Why?"

"The summers of peace and love, right? *For* something, right?"

She smiles. She has a great smile. "Mmm-hmm."

"Didn't do any good, did it? Made no difference at all, right?"

"Michael, I'd love to debate you on that. I'd love to talk about it some more, but my next appointment is five minutes ago."

"Well, that's the way it goes," I say. Two ships passing in the night. I get up to leave. "Thanks, Mrs. Coyle."

"You're welcome. Oh—and Michael, ease up a little on Mrs. Hanover?"

Mrs. Hanover is my dense social studies teacher. "I'm being very good. I'm participating in class discussion, Mrs. Coyle."

"I hear it's more like monologues." Her mouth is twitching like she's trying not to laugh. "You're disrupting her lesson plans."

On my way out, I pass by her next appointment; this kid has junior yuppie I-wanna-get-in-the-Ivies written all over him. I just know I was a touch of refreshment in her long, dreary day.

I'm actually turned on by my *guidance counselor*! She said I was bright, charming, articulate—if we'd had a little more time, maybe she'd have gotten to good-looking. . . . Okay, there's the minor detail of a husband and a couple of little kids. But I have a feeling we'd have something in common. I can picture us having great conversations—right, like in another life.

Listen, something in common has to count. That's why this strikes me so hilarious: Late last night, Johnny came by my house; my high hat was in his van, so he dropped it off. He was way up and raving; seems like he and Jessica got together after the beach and they're going out. Studly Americana and Jessica—how bizarre can it get?

Tom

It's Monday, my worst day because I don't get a free period until 11:45 and by then, my stomach's growling. Thursday is my weird day because I'm free at 9:50 and I don't have another class until 2:00. North Bay High is on modular scheduling, whatever the hell that means. We're supposed to spend our free time in the resource centers. I haven't been inside a resource center since last October. The Out of Control crowd hangs out at the far left corner of the stone wall in back of the school. There's always somebody there, sitting where the wall gets low.

Finally, it's 11:45 and Mod 9 has just ended. I stop at the cafeteria and pick up a bagel and a chocolate doughnut to carry out with me. I'm walking down the path in the back and I can see Mike, Annie, and Dale way down at our spot. The jocks and jockettes are in a cluster close to the back door. I don't like to pass them, because somebody always makes a crack.

"Check out the blimp stuffin' his face!"

I walk by fast. The black kids are to the right. They've got a big box playing rap and two of the girls are dancing on the cracked concrete. I don't know any of the black kids well enough to ask this, but why are they all tuned to rap? How did the race that brought us Charlie Parker, Duke Ellington, John Coltrane et al. wind up with a whole generation of kids turned on by M. C. Hammer? Mike says if he were a black revolutionary, he'd ask some hard questions of radio stations and record companies. Well, I'm just a fat white kid in picturesque North Bay. Okay, I'm not playing jazz, either, I'm playing rock, but Darren's stuff is good, no apologies.

I'm polishing off the bagel. Annie sees me waddling along and waves and I wave back. There's a huge mob of kids out today, all crowded into this little back area of the school; it's a beautiful day and anyway, the indoor smoking lounge has been taken over by the North Bay Mafia. What's funny about all these kids squeezed into this tiny, weedy back area is that North Bay High has a huge lawn in front, perfectly green and beautiful, with great landscaping. Right now, there are flowering fruit trees in bloom—I think they're flowering almond—planted by the Citizens for a More Beautiful North Bay. But we're not allowed to sit on the grass or hang out at the stairs in front of the school because it's right in the center of town. They say it gives the taxpayers a bad impression to see kids hanging around outside. So we're herded to the back, where we're invisible. Keep 'em under wraps, folks. Makes me think of the lyrics for Darren's song.

Out of Control
Rampant and amok . . .

I start to dum-da-dum-dum the bass line, but my mouth is full of chocolate doughnut, so I stop and swallow the last of it.

I'm in an up mood. I give everybody my jolly hello when I get there. I bum a cigarette from Mike and I say, "So, old buddy, what's happening?"

Mike is sitting on the wall and squinting into the sun. "Some news about your friend Johnny."

"What?" I say, and then I hear the words that make the bagel and the doughnut stay stuck someplace in my esophagus.

"Studly Americana and Jessica are going out."

"What?" I repeat.

"How's that for an off-the-wall combination? He asked her out last night and she said yes." He's making a thing of shaking his head like he's clearing it.

I'm fighting to keep my expression cool. "How do you know?"

"Johnny stopped by last night and—get this—he's in love. He was flying! He's saying how he hasn't had a real girlfriend in years and how fantastic she's going to be to go out with, and I'm standing there, trying to keep a straight face. . . ."

I saw how he maneuvered her into his van on the way home from the beach. I knew he'd come on to her sooner or later. But I never thought Jessica would go along with it. Not Jessica!

Mike's laughing. "I give them one, maybe two weeks, tops. They'll be a cute pair, all right."

"Yeah, sure," I say. I have to keep on smiling and listening to him.

"Can you picture their conversations? She'll be talking about nuclear fission and he'll be talking about Budweiser. . . ."

The aftertaste of chocolate icing is turning sour in my mouth.

"We should say something to her. We should warn her—" I say.

Mike shoots me an odd look. "She knows about Studly. It's her choice."

"Yeah, right," I say. What else am I gonna say?

I'm grateful that Dale boosts herself up on the wall next to Mike and they start talking about something else.

Jessica! Oh, Jessica!

I take a long drag on the butt and it burns my throat. I'm leaning against the edge of the wall and it's digging into my back. I almost welcome physical pain, because anything would be better than what I'm feeling.

Jess! Okay, Johnny is the stud supreme. We all know that. He's got something and wherever we go, he can get all the dirtbags he wants. But not Jessica! She's too smart and too classy to ever be interested in him . . . isn't she? God, if I could lose fifty pounds. Because I've got so much going for me. Jessica's said that herself. I know I'm smarter than Johnny, a hell of a lot smarter. I'm talented; I play the bass better than any amateur. I've got personality and I can be very funny, and how many times has Jessie told me that I have a sweet face, that I'd be so good-looking if I'd lose a few pounds. Just a few pounds! I couldn't expect a girl like Jessica to get past the weight . . . or the stretch marks . . . the belts that won't close, the buttons that keep popping . . . the clouds of talc to keep my thighs from chafing. . . . Could any girl? I'm grotesque. I'm the sideshow freak. But I used to think if anyone could get past all that, maybe Jessica could, because she *knows* me. We've been so close, we've had so many deep conversations and shared all those laughs. The time we got stranded on Miracle Mile and . . .

I can't imagine her talking to Johnny about the isolation she feels inside her own family or how a mathematical equation can represent perfect order. Johnny wouldn't understand word one. I enjoyed talking to her and looking at her and walking down the street with a beautiful girl like that. I never risked spoiling it, I never made the slightest move. I guess I had to know there'd be some guy sometime. But of all people, why did it have to be Johnny? He doesn't deserve her! It's not right!

Johnny. We've been friends a long time. Everyone thinks we're so different, but we're brothers under the skin. Whatever grabs him, he has to binge. He's been shaken up by the accident. He says he's not doing drugs anymore. He says he's going to slow up on the drinking. Maybe he can. But I know for sure, because I know Johnny, that there's going to be something else to take its place. Something that he's going to go overboard on. I can't even begin to guess what, but I know for sure there'll be something. And the reason I know is that I'm just like him, only with me, it's food.

One time I was pigging out at a barbecue and I looked up to see Johnny watching me. Barbecue sauce was running down my chin, those spareribs were so great, and I couldn't stop gnawing at the bones. Johnny had that look of recognition in his eyes—one of those "it takes one to know one" looks.

I'm a xanthene addict. Ha, that's the feel-good element in chocolate. Hershey Bar Heaven. I don't stop there. I like the melty texture of cheese in pizza, macaroni and cheese, grilled cheese on toast. And there's something about meatball heroes with peppers, and potato chips with sour cream dip, and for real old-fashioned comfort, there's butterscotch pudding with whipped cream the way Mom used to make. . . . Oh yeah, I know all about comfort food. They sent me to fat-boy camp one summer and I had it all explained to me. Understanding is one thing and stopping is another. I keep ballooning and I'm a brother to all the girls in the crowd.

The only girl I ever screwed was one of Johnny's leftovers. He picked her up at the Three Deuces and we went over to his house. He had her in his bedroom and then he was tired of her. She'd been drinking a lot and she was kind of sloppy and he passed her to me. He gave me a slap on the back and a grin. He thought he was doing me a favor. The longing was overpowering; I had her, too. I had wanted someone for so long; I was going to change her life with kindness, get her off the sauce, treat her with respect, get close to her, inundate her with self-esteem. True Life Romance. When she sobered up a little, she wouldn't come within a mile of me.

I felt sick with disgust for taking Johnny's sloppy seconds. I left Johnny's house and wandered around for a while. I honestly wanted to kill myself. I thought of throwing myself under a truck that was barreling down Shoreview Road and being done with it. So I went over to Baskin-Robbins and had two Super Heaters, with the hot fudge sauce and the nuts and the coconut.

"Hey, Tom!"

It's Jessica. She's out on her free period and she has a big smile, full-strength dimples. She's wearing a bright green T-shirt that matches her streaks. She has the beginning of a golden tan. I can't stand to see her.

"Hi," I mumble and I look away fast.

"Tom?" She sounds a little hurt.

I don't have to turn back. I can ignore her if I want to.

"Tom? Are you mad about something?"

It pours out. "I'm not mad about anything. Just surprised. Surprised and disappointed, that's all. You know, I had more respect for you than anyone I know. But Johnny!"

"You've heard?"

"Mike's blabbing to the whole world."

"I thought you'd say 'congratulations' or something. I thought you and Johnny were such good friends."

"We are. That's how I know he's never going to stick with one girl. You know what he's like. What the hell are you doing, Jess?"

"People change," she says quietly.

"Come on! Johnny's a skeavy guy, that's all. You know how everybody kids around when he's missing. 'If you're looking for Johnny, check out the nearest gutter.' You've heard that yourself."

"He's different with me."

"Yeah. I wonder where he stashed away that blond from the other night."

"That was before—"

"Oh, sure." My tone is as cutting as I can make it. "I never thought you'd be one of Studly's broads. Not you, Jessica."

Her eyes widen. "Tom, he's so nice with me, there's a special feeling between us and—"

"You know how dumb you sound?" How did he get to her? Jessica's so cautious, so afraid of getting hurt. "He'll cheat on you. He's using you."

"You don't know that! You don't know how he is with

me!" I've hit a nerve and she's furious. "And it's none of your business!"

We stare at each other for a moment and then I say, "Look, I love the guy, but— Look, I just wanted to warn you."

"Who appointed *you* my guardian?"

I turn my back to her. I'm not her guardian. I'm not her anything. "Do what you want," I mumble.

I study the trees in the distance.

There is a long pause and then I feel her touching my arm.

"I know you mean well," she says softly. "But I have to see what happens. I have to see for myself. Tom . . . I like him. I really like him."

The touch of her hand on my arm makes me want to cry.

Jerry

I cut my last class at Bartholomew's so that I can get over to North Bay before school lets out. I want to surprise her. I want to see her, see if she still makes me feel that happy. Anyway, it was American studies and I get bored. Who gives a shit about what some dude said in some other century? All I care about is right now. Right now, I want Jessica.

She said she had late classes every day. I get there early and steer the van around the circular driveway. Who was the genius who put blocks all over the driveway? It's stop, go slow, slow, slower, pain in the ass.

There are other cars waiting and I jockey for position. I want to park close to the steps so I can spot her whether she comes out the front or the side. I wind up in the No Standing—School Bus zone, so I keep the motor running. I'm pretty sure she'll see the van whichever way she comes out.

Some kids walk by, but it's still quiet. North Bay hasn't let out yet.

I want everyone to know she's my girlfriend. She's one of the smart kids that get in honors math and all that. Even Mike said she's smart.

The driver ed car goes past, returning from wherever, and lets a bunch of kids out. One of them is a real smart ass, got driver ed on the brain.

"Hey," she yells at me, "bus zone! You can't stay there!"

I'm thinking about how great being in love is, what a high, so why does the whole world want to go and break my mood? I'm not hurting her damn bus zone!

Then—*bang*!—all of a sudden, crowds of kids come pouring out of the doors. There's a lot of noise and yelling, and my head's turning all around looking for her. I don't even know what color clothes she's wearing.

I see her coming from the side, in the midst of the crowd. She's walking along, carrying some books, a real neat-looking chick. Her head's down a little like she's busy thinking her own thoughts, off-guard and sweet. I start to call out, but I'm going to wait. I like watching her like this.

She looks up and sees the van. She stops dead for a second and then she realizes it's me. This big smile breaks out and she's running over to me. It's just the way it was supposed to be, the way she's running right over, happy and excited.

"Johnny! Hi!" She's breathless. "What are you doing here?"

"I came to pick you up."

"I almost didn't see you, I would have missed you—"

"I'm not going to have you *walking* home."

She laughs. "It's only six blocks."

I take her books and toss them in the back. I help her up into the van and the school bus is beeping behind me.

"I'm gonna spoil you," I say. "You'll see." I like the quick-smile way she responds. Nothing's too good for someone that's mine. I'm going to treat her like a queen. I ought to buy her a present, maybe some jewelry, a necklace or something.

We pull out and the bus driver is yelling at me. I start to give him the finger and then I don't bother. Jessica's mine and nothing's going to bug me today.

"Oh, wait," she says. "I'm not going home now. I'm supposed to go straight over to Darren's."

"No one told me about a rehearsal."

"No," she says, "it's just me."

"What for?"

"He wants to work on something with me," she goes. "He didn't say what."

I'm driving slow over the blocks.

"Just you and him, huh?" I glance sideways at her. "Where's your guitar?"

"I left it over there."

"Oh."

Darren's a good-looking dude. He's never acted especially nice to Jessica, but the way it is, everyone wants what I've got. Everyone wants a piece of my action. That's the feeling I get. Mike wants my motorcycle so bad he can't keep his hands off. All of a sudden, all the guys are going to notice Jessica because I picked her out. Tom's the only one I can trust. . . . Hey, maybe Darren really does want to work on something for the band. With Darren, you could have a *Playboy* nude sitting right there and he'd be busy working out some chords. Anyway, he's all tied up with Barbara, right? I'm not going to get uptight imagining things.

"Okay. I'll drive you over to Darren's."

"Maybe you could stay awhile? It's going to be boring for you, but—"

"Sure, I can stay awhile. I have to get over to Mineola later—"

"It might be easier for me. I know where to come in better when I hear the lyrics. You know how he gets, he's so impatient and—"

"No problem," I say. "I'm supposed to pick up something in Mineola for my dad, but it can wait."

"So if you're there to sing the lyric . . ."

"Sure," I say. "I'll help you any way I can."

"Thanks, Johnny."

She leans over and nuzzles against me. Her skin smells like vanilla today.

We're sitting on the orange crates down in Darren's basement. I watch his face to see if he's disappointed that I turned up along with her. But no, no sign.

"I'm glad you showed up," he goes. "You could help."

"What's this all about?" I say.

"I've been thinking about the band getting more visual. Especially Jessica."

"I don't follow you, Darren," she says.

"You're a good-looking girl. You could do more. Think about Madonna, for instance."

"I don't sing," she says. "I don't dance."

"Yeah, but you can move more. You could dress sexier, show a little cleavage, move around. . . ."

She's wearing a loose green T-shirt that pretty much hides what she's got. I think about the way she looked in the bikini yesterday. It's not like she's massive, but she's got a nice shape. I can see what Darren means. Up in front of the band, wearing a real low V, for instance, like down to the waist—she'd get attention for sure. I don't want everyone looking at her, though.

"Darren," Jessica says, "I think I'd rather just concentrate on getting my notes."

He looks disgusted. "Try it, okay? On something like 'Now,' it's all in the lyrics, anyway. Just go with it."

Darren goes over to the keyboards. "All right, come on, let's try it."

"You mean right now?" Jessica says.

"Yeah," he says. " 'Now' *now*."

"Funny," Jessica says. She gets up slow and picks up her guitar.

"Stay there and just run through the lyric," Darren says to me.

"Okay." I'm sitting on the orange crate, leaning my back against the wall.

"Darren?" Jessica says, "I thought we were going to go over the changes in 'Queen of Burger King.' "

"I wrote them all out for you. All you have to do is practice." He starts to play the opening to "Now."

"Where do you want me?"

"Center front. In front of the band."

"But wouldn't Johnny be in front, singing?"

"So you'll get to one side of him. Johnny's all over the place once he gets started. Let's go."

"What exactly do you want me to do?" Jessica goes.

"You want me to get you a choreographer, princess? Just move with the damn song!" Darren starts the opening again. "Swing with it."

"Now" is my kind of tune. I don't like the songs where Darren gets complicated. "Now" is something I can get into. I'm sitting down and singing quietly and watching Jessica. She's trying so hard.

Now I really want to love you
Now I really want to turn you on
Now's the time for me to love you
Now before the magic's dead and gone
Now, baby, now
Right now

Jessica is standing awkwardly and looking at Darren. I thought I'd feel jealous if she started to throw it around, you know, but it's nothing like that. The way she looks reminds me of when I was a little kid, standing up at the blackboard in front of the whole class, with a mistake I didn't even understand, with the teacher looking more and more impatient.

"Smile," Darren says. "Move your hips."

We go on with it.

Now you really want to love me
Now you really want to get it on

"Turn around," Darren says. "Look over your shoulder and swing your hips."

Jessica is moving like a piece of wood. She's forcing her hips to sway, not feeling anything, trying to smile. How can a girl who walks and runs with so much grace look so clumsy?

Now, baby, now
Right now!

I'm still sitting, watching. I give her credit for a lot of guts. The keyboards and the guitar finally come to an end.

No one says anything.

"I'm sorry," Jessica says. Even in this light, I can see the blush spreading. "It's hard for me to concentrate on the notes at the same time."

"They're simple chords," Darren says. "You know them backward."

"Listen, let me try to work something out by myself first."

Jessica hasn't looked at me once since we started the song. She still won't look at me. She looks embarrassed. I'm wondering if my being here, watching, makes it a lot worse.

"In the privacy of your bedroom," Darren says, "you are not going to have me on the keys or Johnny singing the lyrics to you, so could you please try to work something out here and now? Try it again. Try to get into it."

I can't believe him. He's going to make her go through it again! Darren comes on like a sledgehammer.

"This is show business, baby," he says, "so let's show it."

"Okay," she says miserably, and gets into position again.

"Cut it out!" I explode. "Leave her alone!"

Darren swings around. "What's your problem, man?"

Jessica looks at me.

"She doesn't even have the drums or anything! What the hell do you expect her to do?"

"All I'm asking her to do is move with it."

"Give her a chance to warm up a little!"

"Can't I do what I've always done?" Jessica asks miserably. "Can't I just play the damn chords?"

"Oh, shit!" Darren says.

There's a long, dead silence and Darren swivels around on the piano stool. He takes a deep breath and I can see him getting ready to go into his friendly human being routine.

"Okay, guys," he says. "I've got something to tell you. I was going to tell everyone at the same time, but, okay, I'll catch Tom and Mike later."

"What?" I say.

"Sorry, Jess." He smiles at her, but his eyes are cold. I was right. It's his human riff. "Sorry to pressure you like this. The thing is, I'm trying to get a good act together. You've both heard Thin Ice?"

"Sure," I say. "They do 'Fantasy Road.' "

"Yeah," Darren says. "They're on MTV like every day. Someone's pushing them big. Now that's a visual group. Jessica, think about the way Linda Ann Garcia moves on that."

"What's this with you and 'visual' today?" I say.

"A friend of mine knows Dennis Ryan, so I just happened to get introduced to him. Ryan only used to manage Thin Ice back when they were getting started on the Island. He's always looking for other groups and he wants groups that can put on a show. Think visually, Ryan said. Everybody's doing visuals."

"Yeah?" There's something going on. Darren looks like he's jumping inside and having trouble keeping the lid on.

"Ryan loved our demo and he wants to see us. He might even get an A&R man from Columbia to check us out."

"Darren, this is no shit?" I say.

"No shit. The guy's interested."

"Thin Ice!" I say. Up till now, it's all been fun, like a hobby. But wouldn't it be a gas to be successful at something I'm good at! Something that comes so easy, like second nature!

Darren's still talking. ". . . and the one thing we've always needed is a manager and Ryan has all the contacts and . . ."

"Sure, if he managed Thin Ice!"

". . . on the road and get ourselves the hell out of Three Deuces and . . ."

Jessica looks pinched and quiet. "That sounds wonderful, Darren. I don't know that I can do it. . . ." Her voice trails off.

She's probably right. She can't do what Darren wants. She's not Madonna or Linda Ann Garcia, either, that's for sure. She knows it and she's breaking my heart. I put my arm around her.

"So let's try it again," Darren says.

"No," I say. "Let's have a couple of beers first. Okay if Jessica goes upstairs and gets us a couple?" I kind of pinch her shoulder so she'll go without arguing.

It's funny to watch Darren trying to hide his impatience. "Yeah, sure, go ahead," he says.

We watch her go up the stairs and out of sight.

"Listen," I say, "you're making her freeze."

Darren shrugs.

"Let me work with her," I tell him. "I'll get her loosened up and she'll be great."

"If she could *do* a little more—she's the weak link," he says.

"Get off it, Darren," I say. "You gotta be blind. Jessica's the best visual your ugly band's got."

"Maybe. She's pretty enough, but she could use more T and A."

I feel my face getting hot. "You better keep your mouth off her!" I don't like anything of mine put down.

"What's going on?" he says.

I thought he'd know by now. I guess the grapevine's slowing down. "Jessica and me, we're going out."

"Shit!" Darren's upset. He slaps his forehead with his hand. Was he after her or what?

"You got a problem with that?" I say.

"*You've* got the problem! Do you have to go in your own backyard? With your own *band*? What happens when you drop her? Ever think how that affects Out of Control?"

"Wait a minute. No one's dropping nobody."

"Now of all times. This is no time to break in a new guitar! What happens when—"

"I said nothing's gonna happen. This is permanent."

"Permanent? Come on, Studly. How long has it been?"

"Since Sunday night. After the beach."

"What, a day and a half?" He comes up with a short laugh.

"So stop hassling her. Keep on hassling her and we'll both walk."

Darren thinks that over for a minute. "Okay, okay. Maybe you *can* work with her."

He goes back to noodling on the keyboard while we're waiting for her to come back down.

"I love her," I say.

He looks at me over his shoulder, raises his eyebrow, and gives me a quick salute. "Congratulations."

He looks like he doesn't especially care one way or the other. I guess he's not after her. I'm watching him carefully and I don't see any sign. What did I think he'd do, freak?

Later, I drive Jessica home and we talk in the van.

"I know what he means," she goes. "I understand completely. I feel so . . . so dumb, though. I'm glad he didn't make me try it again."

"Don't worry about it. Just stand up there and play the guitar. You're beautiful and you're enough."

"It's not enough. Darren wants a show."

"Screw Darren," I say.

That draws a little smile out of her.

"I put on the show, right, Jess?"

She nods.

"I'll sing the song right at you and you don't have to do a damn thing. Just look at me and react. Relax about it, all right?"

"All right," she whispers.

"All this 'visual' shit, it's only Darren running rampant and amok again," I continue. "I can handle him."

"What did you say to him? When I came back he was being so nice. . . . I guess I take a lot of garbage from him because I have to respect him. He *is* brilliant; he might even be a genius. . . ."

"Listen, nobody hassles my girlfriend, okay? You tell me if someone bothers you and I'll arrange for a couple of broken kneecaps."

"*Kneecaps?*" She starts to laugh.

She looks cute when she laughs. Her nose wrinkles. Her eyes shine green in the daylight.

"Well, whatever you said to Darren—thanks."

I like being in charge, taking care of things for her. "There's nothing I won't do for you," I tell her. "I love you."

Jessica

Johnny wants to meet my parents.

He's full of surprises. This is *Johnny*, Studly Americana. There's something almost old-fashioned courtly about him. Going out of his way to open car doors for me, things like that, are only part of it. He wants to officially meet my parents. I stalled him off for a while. I just feel self-conscious about it.

I told Mom about him. I described the Ocean Point house and the grounds, and the private school (without any details about what Bartholomew's reputation is). I told her about the pool with the waterfall and the silk walls. I pulled out everything that I thought would impress her. (It impresses me, too. It's true, I can't help it. So much of everything, the extravagance of muchness, makes him a glamorous figure.) I carefully left out some salient points. I want her to like him. I really do.

"He's coming over Thursday night," I said. "He thinks you and Daddy ought to meet him. . . ."

"It was his idea?" she asked.

"Yes."

"He sounds like a gentleman," she said. "He *should* come to the house."

"He wants to see my room and my things and the places I've grown up and everything. . . ." I stopped, feeling awkward.

"The windowpane in your room is cracked. We never did call a glazier."

"I don't think he cares, Mom."

"I wish we had at least called a glazier. And the upstairs hall wallpaper is peeling. . . ."

Now we're all sitting in the living room waiting for the doorbell to ring. Our living room doesn't get lived in much—usually we scatter to separate and far corners of the house. Mom and Dad are on opposite ends of the couch, staring blankly into space with nothing to say to each other. I'm in the green chair, watching out the window for his headlights. I feel like part of a posed mannequin family in a furniture display.

I'm really nervous. If Mom *hates* him, that will complicate things. Dad won't have an opinion; he'll go along with Mom. If they're both against him, I'm in trouble.

Johnny's grammar isn't that great and I'm afraid she'll notice. He has kind of a bad speech pattern, I guess. . . . She might think he's too skinny. He's not really *handsome*, not in a classic way like Darren. . . . I don't know why I'm so nervous.

The doorbell rings and I jump.

Johnny's immaculately conservative in a sport jacket worn with casual nonchalance over a polo shirt. He does everything right. He shakes hands with Dad and calls him "sir." He makes small talk with Mom and he's completely polished. Mom looks kind of flustered. Johnny has her enthralled and she never even notices his double negatives. He's perfect. I had nothing to worry about.

After the right amount of time, we go up to my room and close the door, and he drops the super-smoothness with a grin. He starts poking through my things. He looks at *everything*. He studies my posters and my bookshelves. He picks up the stuffed animals on my bed. He looks in my closet and touches my clothes. He even opens my drawers and runs his hands through my underwear. It kind of bothers me. I don't know why, I don't have any secrets, but he's leaving me nothing private.

I can't say anything; I did ask about all the stuff in his room—but only the things that were already out.

When he's finished, we lie side by side on my bed. We don't really do anything—my *parents* are right downstairs—but there's that heat between us. That heat. The air around us is heavy with it. It fills my whole room. It must be going out through the crack under the door and charging the air downstairs. He strokes my arm and I feel electricity jolt to my toes.

After Johnny leaves, I find Mom by herself in the kitchen, drinking coffee. I can hear the canned TV laughs from the den where Dad is watching.

"He has lovely manners," Mom says.

"I thought you'd like him."

"I do. I like him," she says. She takes a small sip. "Too hot. I wish I still smoked. Sometimes I really miss it."

"You mean with coffee," I say.

"Mmm." She sips again and I see steam rising from the cup. "He's very attractive. He seems nice."

"He is, Mom. I like him a lot."

"He's just the kind of boy I'd hoped to see you with. And he's with that group?"

"Out of Control? Yes."

"He seems—well, finer than the others. . . . So this is the first serious boyfriend?" Her face is a little pink.

With a nod, I dismiss my poor tentative tenth grade prom date. She's right. Johnny is different.

"It's so strange. . . . I've been remembering. . . . It's a funny feeling, I can't help but identify . . ."

That's the most open thing Mom has said to me in years. I look at her closely and I realize with a shock: My God, she's lonely. I never thought about what she was doing in the far corners of the house.

Mike

I'm driving Tom home from Darren's in my rattling red bug, from the third late rehearsal this week.

"Darren's pushing too hard," I say. "I've got a history paper due and I can't get up in the mornings anymore."

"You've got to understand him," Tom says. "He wants us to be ready for—"

"I know, I know. Every word out of his mouth is Ryan and Thin Ice."

"I could use something good happening for a change." Tom sounds very down.

"You know what I wonder about?" I say. "Why is Ryan their *ex*-manager? You catch my drift? Like maybe he was their manager *before* they made it big? Maybe it took their new man to bring them up? Maybe they're celebrating night and day that they got rid of him?"

"Darren says Ryan has all the contacts. An A&R guy at Columbia—"

"Darren wants this so bad, it blurs his thinking," I say.

I make a left turn on Bay Road. The motor has developed a wheeze and I don't think it'll last much longer. What I'd really like is a motorcycle like Johnny's.

"I don't know what I'd do," Tom says. "I'm supposed to go to Bard in the fall and—"

"You'd go with Out of Control in a minute and you know it," I say.

"How about you? What if you have to go on the road? Would you drop out of high school?"

"Are you kidding?" Who in his right mind wouldn't go on the road with a rock group? When do you ever get a chance like that? Actually, it's totally unreal. Ryan hasn't even seen us yet. Actually, I always assumed I'd finish high school and go to college. That's what I'm expected to do, according to the grand lockstep plan.

What's so terrible about traveling across the country playing drums and experiencing life? My folks would have cardiac arrest. It's conceivable to get a general equivalency later and go on to college when I'm ready. I probably do want to go to college, if it doesn't turn out to be an escalated version of North Bay High.

Some of the teachers here are actually bright. I'm not including Mrs. Hanover, who thinks the war in Vietnam ended in 1971. She hates my guts for correcting her. I make her nervous; she's not used to someone attentive to her every word. Most of the kids sit there with eyes glazed over. She was droning on about checks and balances and the great two-party system. Hold it, I said, politicos on both sides are just so many sound bites, controlled by the same ventriloquist's hands. I have to give her some credit: She's coping pretty well with the Student from Hell.

It's the principal who's declared war on me. Like about the mohawk. Okay, the reason I got the mohawk in the first place was that there was this all-night party at Johnny's and in the morning I decided to shave. I was slightly blown and the electric razor slipped a bit and went its own merry way up the side of my head. Johnny tried to even it out on the other side, so by the time we got through, I had a mohawk.

I might have let it grow out, but when I came to school,

Dr. Carringham saw me in the hall. *Dr.* Carringham, it turns out, got his PhD from a diploma mill; it's the truth, but no one publicizes it. Anyway, Carringham saw me and said I had to wear a cap to school. He said my haircut would "distract the student body and not be conducive to learning." Basically, what the student body is learning is how to get into each other's pants and I doubt my haircut would be a deterrent. I could have found a lawyer and taken it to the Supreme Court. I wish I'd actually done that, you know, made a stand for my personal freedom against the establishment. But what with finals, etc., coming up, I took the hassle-free way; I got myself a beret. The whole thing was too depressing, so to add a note of levity, I lettered it to match one of my T-shirts—Vampire Lesbians of Sodom, from that old off-Broadway show. Actually, the show was a hoot, but I guess Carringham never heard of it.

Carringham became apoplectic. "What is that, what is that, something about gay rights?"

"Well, no, it's about vampire rights," I said, "and promoting Sodom as the next big vacation spot. . . ." I would have liked to go on, kind of freewheeling on that theme, but Carringham cut me short.

"Take that thing off. Immediately!"

I spent the day beretless. I've been beretless ever since and the mohawk is permanent.

Since then, I've added combat boots and safety pins and they're symbols, not a joke. The whole system is hopeless. It's all empty lip service, reduced to so much gobbledygook: environment, do your homework, peace, AIDS, clean your room, equality, the ozone layer, not in my backyard, animal rights, you better shape up, liberty for all, the best years of your life, and watch out for that mushroom cloud.

Apocalypse is around the corner and complacent suburbia is asleep. Combat boots, ripped clothing, black worn for mourning, the center barely held together by safety pins—symbols of battle and anarchy. I'm the messenger. The ridiculous part is that even punk has lost all meaning—it's become fashion, picked up by teenyboppers. Actually, not in North Bay so much. North Bay is caught up in an old B movie, football games, rah-rah-rah.

With Carringham as our leader, we're all being molded into this great wriggling tractable mass. Prep for the day when we become nice and tractable voters-consumers, and then we can all march lemminglike into the abyss. The funny thing is, no one bothers me; I'm so far out, no one knows where to start with me. Sometimes I even confuse myself.

Actually, the Out of Control posse is a hot subgroup to be in. When you're rockin' 'n' rollin', there's always femmes around.

The band is using that song I wrote, "Botulism in Mom's Apple Pie." I thought my other one was good, too, but Darren nixed it. It was about lobotomies at reduced rates so everyone can get happy, to one of those "forget your troubles, la la la" Las Vegas–type tunes. I have to talk to Darren some more about that one; I still like it. It would have fit right in at that block party.

For some unlikely reason, we got a gig at the Lloyd Hill Neighborhood Association block party. Maybe we got the job because we're cheap or maybe somebody just screwed up. There they all were, decked out in their informal alligator insignias, getting a load on, straining like crazy to have a good time. Your basic tasteful suburban fiesta. Jessica's mother was there, doing the *twist*, staggering a bit and being sixteen again with this glassy laugh. We're playing things like "Out of Control" and "Bag Lady Blues" while they're doing the twist. Strange scene.

Jessica's okay. I like her. If I had a perfectly lacquered iceberg mother like that, I'd dye my hair green, too. Jess thinks she's punk. With her little narrow green streaks and her tiny emerald stud earrings, all to show off the green flecks in her eyes, she looks more like skewed *Vogue*.

Jessica's okay, but I can't understand what got to Johnny like that. He's not what you'd call a deep thinker, but he's got great style. You gotta like someone who operates strictly on the pleasure principle. But all of a sudden, Jessica is the best thing that ever happened to him. I can't see it. There are certain girls that are astounding—a long-haired redhead in my French class, for one thing, and Johnny's stepmother, who looks like a centerfold, for another—but I'd never describe Jessica as more than cute. She's just not that spectacular.

"You think having Jessica prance around in front of the band is going to help us with Ryan?" I say. "I don't see it.

"Suppose Ryan does take us on," Tom says. "It's not like the old days where groups used to make one big record and fly to a couple of concerts in custom jets. They go out on those one-night-stand bus tours now and—"

"Don't sweat it," I say. "Ryan hasn't even seen us yet."

"I know. I was just thinking. Those road tours are supposed to be tough."

"Are you kidding? It'd be a gas! We'd be living together. Did you ever think about that?"

"No."

"Jessica was talking one day, how we should all live in one of those big old Victorian houses down by the waterfront, all of us, like a family. Darren would be the father, he's authoritarian enough, and—"

"Look where you're going! You're gonna ram that Chevy!"

"There's plenty of room!" Maybe Tom's nervous because I just got my license, but then why didn't he get a ride home with Jessica and Johnny? He lives closer to Johnny, anyway.

"Okay, sorry. What about a family?" Tom says.

"Jessica and I had this great conversation. Darren would be the father and Barbara could be the mother. Perfect, huh? She's so nice and calm, and they've been together so long it's boring. You're the kindly older brother that everyone confides in. I'm the crazy eccentric uncle that nobody wants the neighbors to see. Johnny, of course, is the black sheep brother. Jessica is the bratty kid sister. Actually, Johnny and Jessica together seems kind of incestuous—Hey, how about Johnny and Jess? Did you see them tonight, off in the corner? Think they're getting it on yet?"

"Dammit! Watch the damn road!" Tom yells.

He's been on edge like that all night. I wonder what's bothering him.

Jessica

Johnny, Darren, Mike, and I are in Darren's basement again, waiting for Tom. I'm trying to do my French homework. The lighting is terrible and I still have a lot of translation to go.

"That's nice," Johnny says. "Keep right on ignoring me."

I look up at him quickly. He doesn't look like he's kidding.

"I've got to hand this in tomorrow," I say.

"You could at least talk to me," he says.

"I have to get this done." Why can't he talk to Darren or Mike while we're waiting? It's not like he's all alone with nothing to do. I try to concentrate on "Les Jeux Sont Fait," but I feel hemmed in.

"Johnny," I say, "I'll be too tired to do this later. Anyway, there's only three pages to go." I feel like I'm placating a spoiled, sulky child. I've got to finish the French now. After rehearsal, he'll want to park with me somewhere, at least for a while.

When Darren called this rehearsal, I said, "Again? Not another one!"

Darren turned very cold. "Why? Don't you think you need it, princess?"

"Darren, I've got finals coming up and Regents. I've got to get my homework done and—"

"Keep your priorities straight," Darren said. "Out of Control comes first." He wasn't kidding, either.

Darren's been totally humorless since this Ryan thing.

How did I ever get mixed up with all these crazy people?

It's been a strange week. There were all those long evening rehearsals and Johnny has been picking me up every day after school. It's becoming a blur and I'm exhausted. Johnny and I have made out a lot at his house, in his room, in the afternoons. At first, it seemed very peculiar to me, with his stepmother in the house, downstairs somewhere. But he said it didn't matter, she didn't care. "Laurel is always spaced-out anyway."

His room feels like home to me—the gray velvet bedspread over the water bed, the guns on the rack, the lemon smell of furniture polish, disjointed reflections in the mirrored louvers. It's only been a week, but I've been with Johnny so much, in such a concentrated way, and he's given my days a whole different texture. I'm happy—Tom was wrong about him, I know he was—but sometimes I feel everything is happening too fast.

Like that awful afternoon, when I couldn't do the routine Darren wanted. Johnny was so great and I felt *protected* by him, but when he said, "I'd do anything for you. I love you," I wasn't ready for that. I guess Johnny is more intense or more sophisticated than boys I'm used to.

One night, Johnny brought roses, a dozen beautiful red roses with ferns in pale green florists' paper—and suddenly, I became the kind of girl people give roses to! The expression on Mom's face was odd when she saw them—pleased and very sad, all at once. Funny, it's Mom who has been remembering to change the water. They're in a vase on my desk and I look at them when I wake up in the morning. I lie in bed and I think about Johnny. I think a lot about sleeping with him and I wonder if it's as earth-shaking as they say in novels. I wonder what it's really like. "Virgin" is such a foolish-sounding condition.

One afternoon—Wednesday, I think—he gave me a necklace. It's a gold chain with a cute puffy heart.

"I didn't know what to get," he said. "I have terrible taste in jewelry, so I thought I better get something small."

"It's beautiful," I said.

"Do you like it? You don't have to wear it."

"I definitely will," I said. "It's perfect."

I liked that he wasn't that sure of his taste, so I hugged him, and then he said, "It's to remind you all the time, even when I'm not around—I love you." I stopped in midhug. I don't know. I got that nervous feeling again.

I can't concentrate at all. I translate one more sentence and then I give it up. Mike is arguing with Darren again and he's too loud. It's impossible to do homework here.

"Of all the numbers to pick," Mike is saying, "why 'Now'? It doesn't say a thing."

"Because it's the most commercial—"

"It's a piece of shit and you know it, Darren."

"That's the kind of song Ryan wants, something easy to relate to," Darren says. He sounds less forceful than usual. He must be tired, too.

"I say we work on 'Moral Majority,' " Mike says. He starts to chant the lyric, fingers snapping, his whole body bouncing with it.

The moral majority seeks Satan in strange places

Playing records backward—shows you where their taste is
They'll ban 'n' burn your books, regulate embraces
And tie up all your thoughts in ironclad straight laces. . . .

"We ought to do that and then 'Out of Control' and—" Mike is saying.

Johnny is next to me with his arm around me. "I never really got that," he says to me. "Ironclad straight laces?"

"As in straightlaced," I tell him. I feel faintly embarrassed for him. I mean, he's been singing that lyric for months now.

"Oh. Yeah."

Mike is in midspeech. ". . . and if you sell out, what's the point, Darren? You want to be a bubble gum band?"

" 'Now' is the most commercial—"

"Who cares about commercial?"

"Grow up, Mike. Either we make it now or it's all over. If Ryan doesn't take us on, we've got nothing. Nada. Zilch. There's the North Bay prom and one night at Three Deuces and that's it."

"If all we do is shit like 'Now,' who cares if we fold or not?"

"Wait a minute," Johnny says. "I like it. That's my kind of song."

"Yeah, Johnny. Sure, Johnny," Mike says.

"What's wrong with it?" Johnny says.

"What's wrong with it," Mike says, "is that sex isn't the answer to everything."

"Yeah? Whatever makes me feel good is the answer."

"Feeling good isn't everything in life."

"What's more important than that?" Johnny says.

"I can think of a lot of things more important—"

"Come on," Johnny says, "I know you. Sex and grass are on top of your list."

"You don't know me. That's too simple," Mike says. "What about you, Darren? What's important? Name the three things that come first. . . ."

Darren gets dragged into it and we wind up each taking a scrap of paper. We're each going to write down the three most important things in our lives and then compare them. It's one of those time-killing games we play a lot while we're waiting to go on or waiting for someone to show up.

"Where's Tom, anyway?" Mike says.

I'm chewing on the pencil stub, thinking about what to write.

"He said he'd be late," Darren says.

"I know what Tom would put down." Mike is laughing. "Number one: food."

I look up at Mike. "You keep saying things like that in front of him. It hurts his feelings."

"No it doesn't. He always laughs. . . . What are you gonna put down first, Jessica? 'Feelings, feelings, feelings'?"

I think carefully. Our ground rules are absolute honesty and no jokes. I look over at Johnny. I've seen his writing; he prints in crooked, childlike letters. He's frowning a little and some of his hair has fallen over his forehead. I look at him and I think of sex.

I've lined up the numbers in a neat column. Finally, I write "1. Love (Guys)." That covers Johnny and dating and sex and all future loves in one package. "2" is

"Friends." I'd be a cipher if I didn't have real friends like Annie, Tom, and Dale who I can talk to about almost anything. I think about "3." This isn't that easy. Finally, I decide on "Health," because I think of how good it feels to run when everything is working right, how I couldn't stand it if my body wasn't functioning. I'm going to quit smoking soon.

"Okay. What have you got?" Mike says to me.

"Somebody else first," I say. I feel like biting my nails. I don't always like games like this. Sometimes they expose too much.

Darren shrugs. "I don't care. I'll go first."

He wrote "1. Music, 2. Family, 3. Money."

"You're still my man!" Mike is exuberant. "Music first! Music over bread! You're not a complete grubber yet."

I'm a little surprised at his list and I blurt out, without thinking, "What about Barbara?"

"Oh, shit," Darren groans. "I forgot about her."

There's a silence and I feel bad, really bad, for Barbara. They've been together for almost two years. She's spent so much time waiting around the piano. Even the North Bay graduation prom! She must have been looking forward to that—and Darren took the job, playing for his own prom! Mike and I don't care, because we're not seniors. Johnny goes to Bartholomew's, so it's not his prom, either. Tom was probably relieved—he doesn't have to worry about getting a date now. But how does Barbara feel?

"Listen," Darren says, "this was confidential. Nothing leaves this room, Jessica."

"I'd never say anything."

"You better not or I'll get my walking papers."

Mike is next. He's fairly predictable. He reads, "One. Complete Freedom, Two. Awareness, Three. Integrity. I'm not sure about the exact order but—"

"What's that 'complete freedom'?" Johnny interrupts. "This was supposed to be something personal."

"Asshole," Mike says. "What's more personal than your freedom?"

And now Johnny. He wrote, "1. Jessica. 2. Jessica. 3. Jessica."

Everyone looks at me. I guess I'm pleased. Any girl would be, wouldn't she? I'm always amazed about how open Johnny can be with his feelings and that's really nice, isn't it? I'm proud, too, especially after all those warnings—so why do I suddenly feel trapped? There *has* to be something else in Johnny's life.

Jessica

Johnny's pool has been filled. It's great to come here after school on a hot day.

Johnny and I are in the water. We've been playing, diving and splashing. That's another thing I like about Johnny. He can get into just playing—we've been acting like third graders, having fun and being silly.

Darren and Tom are in the shade, sitting in the chairs on the far side. Tom is all covered up with a T-shirt and a towel; he must be roasting. Darren is talking to him very seriously. Even in a bathing suit, even flaked out on a chaise, Darren never looks completely relaxed. Johnny and I were having this terrific water balloon fight and every once in awhile, Darren shot us a look like we were too childish and noisy.

Now Johnny and I are pretty much worn out and we're resting side by side, elbows propped up on the edge, our legs trailing in the water. We're near the waterfall and I feel a misty spray from it.

"This is heaven," I say.

"It'll get even nicer." The way he's grinning is contagious. "In the summer, they go up to Vermont every weekend, so we'll have the house to ourselves."

"Oh?"

"And they take a lot of three- and four-day weekends. We'll go out on the boat and we'll use the pool, and we'll order dinner in and fool around a lot. Are you gonna like that?"

He knows it makes me self-conscious when he gets direct like that and he laughs at me.

He goes on. "And we'll throw some massive parties. It's all ours from now to fall. You may as well keep some clothes here and—"

"Johnny, my mother expects me to come home sometimes."

"Your mother's got a soft spot for me. If you're with *me*—just tell her, she'll let you stay."

"No way. You don't know my mother."

"We'll work it out. We've got to get rid of your curfew."

"When school's over, maybe she'll make it later. . . ."

"She likes me. I'll talk to her."

"What do you think you're going to say?"

"I don't know. I'll pull some strings."

"Oh sure, Johnny. All you have to do is pull some

strings!" Sometimes he's so sure of himself! I flick my hand in the water and splash him.

"Cut it out," he says. He pulls his hand back, poised and ready to splash.

"No, don't. No more."

"You started up! People that live in glass houses, Jess—"

"Don't you ever go to Vermont with them? It sounds nice, with the lake and—"

"It's boring in the summer. I'll take you there to ski. Hey, can you ski?"

"Pretty well."

"Pretty well. What does that mean?"

"I've gone twice."

He laughs. "I can picture you. Schuss-booming down some hill, not knowing how to stop—"

"You've got it," I say.

"I'll teach you how," he says. "Reckless Sadie, over here."

"People that live in glass houses," I say, and we both smile. It's nice. We really know each other. "Why don't you like it in the summer?"

"Because my dad plays farmer and it's boring."

"Farmer?"

"We've got a lot of acreage and it's supposed to be like a working farm, but it isn't really, and—"

"I thought it was just a house at a lake and—"

"No, it's a farm."

"You mean with *animals* and everything?"

"There's a couple of horses and now they've got this flock of special goats. They're trying to make this goat cheese, because my dad liked some cheese when they were on vacation in Greece and—man, if they ever get it going, it'll be the world's most expensive cheese!" He laughs. "It's my dad's toy. It's rough up there, too, you know what I mean, rustic. He's sunk a fortune in it. We could have had a fleet of Maseratis for what he's putting in those goats. . . ."

I wonder what his father's like. I'm going to meet him at Johnny's graduation.

". . . and now Laurel thinks it would be cute if they had rabbits, so they're getting some this weekend."

"Rabbits? Does somebody feed all those animals during the week?" They sound so—careless—with things.

"Oh, sure. There's a caretaker lives in one of the buildings and my dad and Laurel go up every weekend and play farmer."

"Wow. Sort of like Marie Antoinette," I say.

"Who?"

"You know, Marie Antoinette, playing shepherdess at Hameau, remember?"

"Remember what?" he says. "Who're you talking about?"

"Don't they teach the French Revolution at Bartholomew's?"

"Oh, that. Yeah, sure."

I'm sorry it ever came up. I look at Tom across the pool and I'm glad he's too far away to hear us.

Jessica

This is the best day. I had my Math 11 Regents this morning and I think I did very well, even though I've been so tired all week. I still have the Chemistry Regents coming up and then school is over for the summer. Finally!

Johnny picked me up and drove me to school this morning. That was sweet of him. Bartholomew's is finished now and all he has coming up is his graduation. He could have slept late, but he picked me up at 8:30 and then waited for me the whole time I was taking the test. I didn't want him to. I was going to have lunch with some of the girls afterward. I haven't been alone with my girlfriends for a while and they were all going to King's for egg rolls. I guess I could have asked Johnny to come with them, but we get along best when it's just the two of us. Johnny likes to have my total attention.

During the test, I felt uncomfortable, knowing he was waiting. I didn't rush, but I didn't go over my answers a second time, either. He hung out in back with some kids he knew for part of the time, but basically, he killed two hours. While he was waiting, he took a walk to the card shop and bought me another present.

It's a little red satin heart with arms stretched out on either side, with "I love you this much!" in big white letters. He looks happy about surprising me, watching my face for my reaction. It is extraordinary to feel that someone is thinking of me, aware of me, all the time.

"I never expected you to be like this," I say.

"Like what?"

"You're so nice to me."

"Of course I am," he says. "Why wouldn't I be?"

"Oh, you know the way everyone talked," I say. "All that Studly Americana stuff. And you turned out to be so different."

Big smile; he likes hearing this. He likes being talked about. Johnny did this, Johnny did that, Johnny the center of attention. I like hearing it, too; I'm the girl who had the power to change him.

I go on. "Dale used to tell me you're not capable of loving anybody, all of that." We're smiling into each other's eyes. "And now she's amazed. And Mike says I've really calmed you down."

"When did he say that?"

"A while ago. You know what he wrote in my yearbook? 'Good luck with Johnny, you'll need it.' "

We both laugh because we're so far beyond that.

"Being in love is the best high," he says. "And like they say in Texas, too much ain't enough!"

Jessica

I knew it was coming. I kept thinking about what it was like for everyone else, about what it would be like for me. I even got to the point of watching a teacher in front of the class, so calm and in control, and trying to imagine her actually doing it, carried away, stripped of the civilized veneer. I tried to imagine myself that way.

It seemed like everyone but me was doing it. It was in every song, every movie. I was thinking about it all the time.

I knew Johnny couldn't do anything halfway for very long. Maybe that's what made me follow him down the beach that first day.

I really wanted to. And I was scared stiff.

It was the second weekend that we had the house to ourselves. We made out in the Jacuzzi for hours that afternoon and Johnny kept urging me. So I said okay. Johnny knows how to be abandoned and free, I thought, and I'll learn from him. We had gone awfully far, anyway; it wouldn't be that different.

We went into the house and Johnny laughed when he saw how stiff and shaky I felt. He gave me a piña colada, which is my favorite drink, except that I don't drink in the afternoon. He laughed and said that I looked as if I were facing an operation.

"It's okay," he said. "It's new to me, too. I was never anybody's first before."

I sipped the drink and relaxed—up until I saw him getting prepared. At first, it wasn't all that different from the way I had felt before, but then he became urgent and he forgot to be gentle with me and it hurt. I was trapped, pinned under him. I wanted to say, "No. Wait. I'm not ready for this!" It *hurt*, and then, just as I was beginning to feel something again, it was over too fast. His face was wide open and unguarded and he was saying, "I love you," and I felt like crying. I had crossed a bridge and I wasn't sure that it was worth it. I wasn't sure I had really wanted, truly, in my heart, to do it; maybe I had been mostly curious. Now I wanted to be a little girl again, in smooth white pajamas on freshly laundered sheets, alone and talcumed and cool on a hot summer night. "You belong to me," Johnny said. I heard—no, I *felt* the whirring of wings, beating against a cage.

"It gets better," he said. "They say the first time isn't that good."

"You've got to relax," he said.

"We have to get you on the Pill," he said. "It's much better that way. I'll drive you to that Planned Parenthood place in Mineola and—"

Later, we ordered pizza for dinner and Johnny answered the door with a towel wrapped around him. We ate in bed with the whole length of our legs touching under the cover and he fed me bits of sausage. We got tomato sauce and cheese on the sheets, but it didn't matter because the sheets were pretty much messed up, anyway. And I thought, cuddling was the best part.

Then we watched some of *A Clockwork Orange* on the VCR, but just after the "Singing in the Rain" assault scene, we did it again. We flowed together and this time, it started easy and playful and Johnny took his time. At first, it wasn't all that different from the way I had felt before. There wasn't any earth-shaking difference—and then, suddenly, without warning, I was caught in a whirlpool, going round and round, going under, terrified of drowning. I tried to hold back, but it was too late. Jolts of electricity charged through me, I dug into his shoulder, I shattered. Then it was over and I had somehow come through to the other side.

For once in my life, I had let myself go and I am still here.

"So it wasn't too terrible?" he says.

"No, not too terrible." I think my smile matches his.

If Johnny knows anything at all, he knows the varieties of lovemaking. And I've instinctively picked him as my expert guide.

"I love you!" I say, for the first time on my own initiative instead of just in response to him. I'm warm and glowing, rosy inside and out, every nerve tuned to Johnny.

I don't have the slightest idea of what love is really supposed to be, but this must come close.

Jessica

I keep putting off going to the Planned Parenthood place and Johnny keeps bringing it up. He says it'll be much better for both of us if I'm on the Pill.

"Okay," I say. "Next week. I'll go next week."

"Why not today? Tomorrow?"

"I'll see."

"Yeah, I know," he says. "When you say 'I'll see,' that means the tenth of never."

"All right. Definitely next week."

"Look, I'm not forcing you . . . but it's the difference between skinny-dipping and going in the pool with all your clothes on."

"But they're going to examine me! That's what I heard they do. Somebody with a rubber glove . . ."

"Jess, it's a *doctor*."

It makes me shudder. I can't help it.

Johnny sees. "Okay, little girl. Forget it."

But then, of course, I think about it some more. The Pill would be safer and, Johnny says, a lot better. He's right. I'm being childish.

The next day, Johnny and I are sitting side by side on the waiting room couch of the birth control center. Maybe I should have come here with another girl. Annie would understand how much I dread this. I do appreciate Johnny's willingness to go through this with me.

"Are you cold?" Johnny asks.

"No," I answer, puzzled, and then I realize that I've unconsciously folded my arms in front of my chest, hugging myself. I unfold them and Johnny takes my hand.

"Don't look so sad," he says.

"I'm not."

"I'm with you."

"I know." I've never felt closer to anyone.

"Hey, I love you," Johnny says.

"I love you, too." I try to smile, but my teeth are chattering.

The examination isn't the nightmare I expected. The doctor is a woman, very attractive and soft-spoken. Everything is matter-of-fact. I'm there for medical advice; she'll give me medical advice. I want birth control; she'll give me birth control. I notice that there's a little gray hair mixed with blond, pulled straight back off her forehead. She's nice. It's not her fault that I feel so guilty and embarrassed.

When I have to lie down on the table and put my feet up in the stirrups, I clench my teeth and look at the ceiling.

"Relax," the doctor says. "This won't take long."

When Johnny touches me, it feels so right. More than right. Here I feel the coldness of metal and the strangeness of the gloved hand. It hurts a bit. I concentrate on the ceiling and avoid looking at the doctor. I try to will myself outside my body. Well, if I'm old enough to sleep with Johnny, I'm old enough to survive a pelvic examination! The way Johnny makes me feel is worth all of this. Finally, it's over.

I sit across the desk from the doctor and she gives me a quick rundown of methods. I want the Pill. Then a few questions. The zinger is "Do you smoke?"

"Yes," I say.

"How much?"

"About a pack a day. A little under a pack."

"If you take the Pill, you should keep your smoking down to ten." She goes on about complications, blood circulation, risk of heart trouble. . . ."

"I was planning to quit, anyway," I say.

"I hope you do. For your general health, too."

I tell Johnny about it in the car on the way home.

" '. . . no more than ten cigarettes per day . . .' What if I lose count? Johnny, I'm going to get paranoid about this. If I have eleven cigarettes, I'll be looking for cancer symptoms."

"Come on, Jessica."

"It's a chemical. I'm taking a chemical into my body."

"So?"

"So it scares me."

We drive in silence for a while. I wonder if he knows that I'm on the verge of backing out.

"Johnny, can't we go on the way we have been?"

"You don't want the Pill?"

"I don't know. I don't think so. Why can't sex be simple?"

"It can be, very simple. We can go natural. Nothing to worry about. I got myself tested for AIDS that time I was in the hospital, you know, after the crash. So . . ."

"We have to use *something.*"

"Look, if all this birth control stuff spoils things, we'll take our chances."

"That's crazy. I could get pregnant!"

"What if you do? Hey, Jess, it could be nice. I always wanted a lot of kids. Maybe five."

"Be serious."

"I am. We'd get married a little sooner, that's all."

I look at him incredulously.

"I'm graduating and I'll be working for my dad. No problem."

"But I'm not graduating yet and I'm going on to college and . . ." College, then my own apartment, a job in the city, new people . . . I never thought of Johnny and me beyond right now. We're in different places. He's settling into his real life! I haven't even started mine.

Johnny goes on talking, about when we get married. Not if, *when.* He's daydreaming out loud, enjoying how it's going to be, and I'm in the center of his daydream. I guess that's a nice place to be. Johnny keeps surprising me. I never would have expected him to fantasize about some large, cozy family.

"Anyway," he finishes, "I like babies."

"I never see you playing with your little brother."

"That's different. I'm talking about *our* babies."

"All five of them?" I can't believe he's saying these things.

"Yeah, five of them. Why not?"

"Johnny, I'll go on the Pill. I was going to try to quit smoking, anyhow." The Pill has to be less hazardous than childbirth. Or abortion. Or marriage.

"Okay. You know what? I'll quit with you."

We smile at each other, united in the good fight against Nicotine. It makes me giggle.

"So, you're all set then," he says. He takes a hand off the steering wheel and brushes it lightly against my crotch. It's playful, it's over my jeans, it's in the middle of traffic—but suddenly I am a little group of iron filings jumping, leaping to a magnet.

Nothing needs to be said. He's picking up speed, we're racing toward his house, both of us praying that Laurel won't be home. I recognize the look on his face. The space around us is charged.

This is the way it's been. That first hurried and awkward time seems an eternity of sensation ago. Johnny has been peeling layers of my reserve, leaving me raw and quivering. None of the mechanics, the Pill, methods, science—none of it can spoil this mystery that makes us rush toward each other.

The trouble with Jessica is she's still too immature. She can't understand how deep my feelings for her go. Someone that's been around more would appreciate all this love I've got to give her. I want to be with her all the time and you'd think she'd appreciate that. Like last Saturday. She wanted to spend the day shopping with Annie at Miracle Mile. I just wanted to be alone with her in the house. Finally, I said okay, I'd drive them over, and she said no, she'd get nervous about trying things on if she knew I was standing around, waiting. Why'd she want to be with Annie more than me? I can't figure that.

Or I'm on the phone with her and she says she has to get off and study for a Regents or something. That bothers me. I was talking about the new Corvette I'm getting. I want a black one this time, because that's a classy look, but I'd have to special-order it and I'd have to wait for it. Or I can get one from the showroom right away, but it's blue. I'm talking over this problem with her and she's thinking about some Regents! It used to be that if I called some girl, she'd be jumping with joy right over the phone wires—Johnny calling! But then, I never gave a damn before and I never got around to calling that much.

The thing with Jessica is, I always want to see her *now* and she thinks tomorrow is good enough. I've got to see her when I want to and she doesn't understand that it's because of all this love I have for her.

Like we'll be at a party and she'll be bopping all over the place, talking to everyone in the room, and I do a slow burn. I wind up getting a little drunk and I tell her it's her fault, because of the way she's acting. One time, she got into a long, long conversation with Tom and forgot all about me.

"You're kidding!" Jess goes. "Tom's just about my best friend. Why can't I talk to him?"

"A guy shouldn't be your best friend," I tell her. "It don't look right. Why can't you stick with girlfriends?"

"Johnny, you can't be jealous of Tom! I mean, really, *Tom*!"

She's got a point. "It's not that," I say. "You forgot I was even there."

"You could have joined in the conversation. I don't understand your problem."

"That's because you're too immature," I say. "When you grow up more, you'll understand how to act."

"Oh wow, Mr. Maturity!" and she's smiling that way, you know, the way that melts my bones, and I can't stay mad at her.

I like to be alone with her. The only time I'm sure she's all mine is when we're making love. When she acts like she's slipping away, like at a party or something, I get this shaky feeling. I figure maybe it's because I'm the first one and she needs more time to learn how to be.

I try to explain the way I feel. I keep saying "I love you." I wish I could use words the way Darren does; I'd write her some lyrics. She makes me happy. I don't even drink that much anymore, only if I go out with the guys after her curfew. All I need is Jessica.

So I've been feeling a lot better in the mornings and

maybe I'll get back in shape. I'm gonna try to gain back the weight I lost when I was on that speed kick. I don't even know why I did that. I guess because I can't handle not being happy. I don't need it now. Almost the only thing I do is a little snow, maybe, at a party, and that's once in a blue moon. All I need is Jessica.

We have fun times. She can laugh so hard and so long, when something strikes her funny. We've laughed together at things until the tears started rolling down.

She likes the motorcycle; she hangs on to my waist for dear life and yells at me to go faster, over bumps, like some excited little kid. She didn't want to wear the helmet because it's so heavy and I told her she had to. I feel good taking care of her like that.

She's just learning to walk in high heels. I don't know where she's been, it's like she's spent her whole life in jeans and I'm beginning to take her places where she has to dress. So she takes a deep breath, hangs on to my arm, fakes this very sophisticated expresison to make an entrance, and in the meantime, her ankles are turning. She has terrible table manners, too. In a restaurant, she'll be on good behavior and spend an hour turning spaghetti around her fork, giving me this "aren't you proud of me?" look. When it's just the two of us, at my house, she'll eat spaghetti out of the can with her hands. I like all those things because it's Jessica. Like, I'm never gonna want a chick with normal, long nails. It doesn't sound like much when I tell her in my own words. If I was Darren, I'd write her a poem.

I wish I could remember a poem I heard. It was something about dark red roses standing for blood and passion. It was symbolic and she likes things like that.

Sometimes I bring her roses, when I'm passing her house in the morning, even if I know she's at school, just to surprise her when she gets home. Her mother and me get along fine. I always bring red roses, two of them, with ferns, and her mother gives me this little vase. I fill it up with water at the kitchen sink, and her mother leans against the counter, watching me and smiling like I'm doing something great. We talk and she likes me to stay and have coffee with her.

I take the flowers upstairs and put them on Jessica's desk. I leave those little florist's cards around for her to find. I stand one up against the vase and tuck an extra one in her bed, under the quilt. If I could remember that poem, I'd write it for her. Instead, I write "I love you" and "I love you again." I like surprising her like that. And I want her thinking about me all the time, even when I'm not there.

It's been great. Jessica's eyes are green fire when we make love. We've been in the living room and on the water bed and the best was one warm night, in the pool, in the moonlight, under the stars. I'm like crazy, wanting to break down all her barriers. Her skin smells like vanilla. I can't love her enough. I taste her dimples, the pulse point at her neck, the pink nipples, every hollow and crevice, and I can't love her enough. She's so beautiful, inside and out. I keep driving to reach her very center and one day, there's going to be nothing else for her but me.

Jessica

I should be happier. I do care for Johnny and Mom talks and talks about how wonderful he is to me, and that's true. But I wish she wouldn't talk about it so much. For once, I have her stamp of approval—but can't she *see* how Johnny is? I don't know, suddenly she's too enamored with the roses, the presents, the romantic touches.

He calls me all the time and when I'm not home, she takes the message. I don't always feel like calling him back right away.

"But Jessica," she says, "he's waiting for your call!"

"I'll call in a minute," I say. "I just need a chance to breathe."

"But he said to call immediately—he's been trying to reach you for hours—"

I marvel at his ability to get Mom caught up in his urgency. He makes everything urgent; he has to talk to me right away, he has to see me, it has to be tonight, not tomorrow. Whatever Johnny wants becomes an emergency. And he wants me *all the time*!

Johnny loves with open arms, he surrounds me with love, he overwhelms me with love. He's made me much more sure of myself, even performing in front of the band. The green streaks are growing out and I don't think I'll even bother to put them in again. They used to make me feel avant-garde and uninhibited—and now they seem silly. I just don't need them anymore—not for the band, not for myself. Johnny reminds me that I'm desirable, lovable, even spectacular. Things couldn't be more perfect. That's why I feel so guilty sometimes. I should be happier.

Maybe I'm too tired and irritable because of all of Darren's rehearsals. Maybe I'm not as intense as Johnny.

Maybe I was doing an experiment with the fusion of our lips, the meshing of our bodies—and suddenly, it's not that simple.

Darren

It's only 9:30 and it's hot already. It's going to be a bitch of a day. I don't have to be at work until ten and I'm sitting on the bleachers near the high school track, drinking coffee out of a cardboard container from the deli.

I'm sitting on the third rung of the bleachers, looking out at the field. Through the early morning haze, I watch the runners on the track. Some old guy, lean and stringy-muscular, jogging slow but steady. At the far end, a girl in white shorts, fast, nice body from here. Two young boys on bikes, weaving on and off the track, raising little clouds of dust. It looked so different a couple of days ago. The graduation was held here. There were rows of chairs on the field and the bleachers were jammed. It was hot that day, too. I wore shorts under the black robe.

Mom was there, with Frankie and George. Out of Control was there, too: Tom next to me in the line of graduates, Mike playing drums in the school band and trying to give his individual beat to "Pomp and Circumstance," Johnny and Jessica watching from the bleachers. A big crowd.

I got the Donald K. Loring Award for Excellence in Stage Band, sandwiched between the Latin Club Commendation and the Graphic Arts Award. Whoopee, and who the hell was Donald K. Loring, anyway? I saw Jessica and Johnny cheering wildly. Mom was happy and Mike did a big drum roll when they announced my name, which made me laugh and drew a dirty look from the principal.

I turned and looked at Barbara a row behind me—just out of habit, I guess. She stared back at me, looking solemn in the black robe. That reminded me, fast, like a punch, that we're through. The curve of her cheek looked especially soft against the stark black and I suddenly longed for her, almost the way I used to in the beginning. I wish she had at least smiled, but she just stared at me until I turned away.

I can see why she gave up on me. Working on prom night was only the last of many straws. I know it was my fault, but I can't be any different. I look down at the coffee left in the container and I feel my life going nowhere.

Waiting for Ryan. Waiting for Ryan. I ought to put it to music. It has a ring to it. Waiting for Ryan. Makes me think of that play we read in World Drama, *Waiting for Godot*. Two bums waiting for something that never comes and never will. And I'm waiting for Ryan to save my life.

Waiting for Ryan or waiting for Godot
Your dreams got to have someplace to go. . . .

I've got to stop thinking in lyrics all the time! He was going to hear us this week, so I rehearsed the guys until they were ready to drop. We were up for it and then he canceled. Now he says he'll come by for our gig at the Three Deuces and that's not until near the end of July! He wants to see us in action, in front of an audience. I wonder if he's really going to come all the way out to North Bay. My friend says he liked our demo a lot.

So here I sit, high school graduate, proud possessor of the Donald K. Loring Award and about to go to work cleaning walls and desks in the high school.

It's not bad. It leaves my afternoons free to practice or sleep, and the nights free for gigs or Barbara. Dammit, forgot again, no Barbara. And it gives me plenty of time to think. I do the scrubbing mechanically and only notice what I'm doing when I come across an obvious Mike line—ANARCHY FOR THE UK—scrawled on the wall in distinctive purple marker. Mike says he's creating summer jobs.

The girl in white shorts is running closer, great pair of legs and—it's Jessica! When she comes near my end, I call out "Jess!" She waves without breaking stride. Then I see her slow down at the entrance to the track. She picks up an Adidas bag from the grass and walks over to me. Close up, I see her face is dripping wet, even with the white sweatband.

"Hi, Darren," she pants, sinking down on the wooden slat below me.

"I was just saying hello, I didn't mean to stop you," I tell her.

"I was quitting anyway. I did two miles." She's unzipping the athletic bag. She pulls out a towel and wipes her face. "I used to be able to go and go."

"I didn't know you ran."

"I used to, in junior high. I'm trying to get back to it. I don't know, it makes me feel a lot better."

"Better than what?"

"I don't know. Running makes me feel free." She shrugs and laughs. "What are you doing up so early?"

"Working."

"Oh, right," she says. "At the school."

"I don't start till ten, but I get a ride over with my mom on her way to work. I could've used the extra half hour sleep this morning."

"How late did everyone stay?"

"I don't know. Mike and Chris were still in the basement when I went upstairs. . . . You were good last night. A whole lot looser."

She smiles, pleased. "Thanks. It's coming easier. I've been practicing so much." She puts the towel around the back of her neck. "You know, with this Ryan thing, I know I'm not really on that level. I've been worrying that you might want to replace me. . . ."

"I gave it some thought."

She looks up at me quickly. "You did? Was I that bad?"

"No. It's just that you and Johnny—well, I thought it would be Johnny's usual scene and if there were hard feelings— We can't do without Johnny, so I was trying to think of guitarists."

"Oh, great!"

"Just as a backup. Listen, it's worked out fine. Who'd believe you'd even get him to rehearsals on time! So there's no problem, right?"

"You're all heart, Darren."

"Yeah, those were Barbara's last words, too. I know, I'm always the heavy. Can't anybody understand I've got one friggin' summer left? The rest of you don't give a damn. One extra rehearsal and everybody screams! And you had to go and get involved with someone in your own band. You don't do that, that's not too bright. What if it hadn't worked out, what would that do to the band? Ever consider that?"

"You're cute, Darren. Your concern for me is touching."

"Come on, Jess. It's nothing personal." Maybe I was being too honest again.

Now she's taking a little can of orange juice out of the bag and frowning, working on pulling up the tab. "You're making too much hinge on one summer, Darren."

She doesn't understand. I've got to set a time limit. I've got to see something happening or I've got to do something else.

"I've got too many responsibilities to keep chasing rainbows," I say.

"You sound like some middle-aged married guy with ten kids."

"I've got my mother and brothers to consider."

"Hey Darren, you're only eighteen."

"Yeah, I know." I watch her drinking from the can. What does Jessica know about the real world? Mom tries to hide how rough it is. She's drained from pinching pennies, overwhelmed by responsibility, trying to cope with George and Frankie all by herself and then one unexpected thing, one extra bill—the damn plumbing, last week—and I see her fighting not to fall apart. All

Jessica has to think about is where the next party's going to be.

"You know what's wrong with you, Darren?" she says.

"No, tell me, what's wrong with me?"

"Seriously," she says. "You want a guarantee on a silver platter. You can't ever know how things will work out."

"I can't afford any risks," I say.

"Life's supposed to be an adventure. It shouldn't be some lockstep preplan."

I laugh. "You've been talking to Mike. 'Gray drones marching to and from the LIRR in lockstep.' "

"That sounds like Mike, all right." She laughs, too.

"I'll leave the adventures to Johnny. He's always got the old man's dough to bail him out."

"You're so wrong! Johnny has the courage to take chances."

"So he gets drunk and wrecks cars."

"He doesn't do that anymore! He really doesn't drink much anymore."

I shrug.

"He plunges into things, totally," she says. "He doesn't hold anything back, no safety nets ever. If you want music that much, go for it, no matter what. Johnny would. That's what I call courage."

"I'd call Johnny compulsive," I say. I wonder how much she knows about Johnny last summer. He sure plunged into partying, totally.

"He gives *everything*. He's even that way with an audience, you've seen him. He'd never think of bailing out."

"He's not that way as a matter of philosophy," I say. "It's mostly off-the-wall."

"Johnny has enormous capacity for feeling. That's not off-the-wall! That's what makes him so wonderful."

"I've known him a long time," I say. "He always has to be flying high about something. He specializes in crash landings."

She looks uncomfortable.

"Jess, this is just talk," I say. "I like him a hell of a lot. He's a great guy."

"He is, isn't he?" She smiles automatically, like someone who's been told too many times what a pretty smile she has. "This is some conversation. It must be too much morning air."

"Yeah," I say.

What's going on? Maybe Johnny's getting compulsive about Jessica, who the hell knows. I just hope they hold it together until Ryan gets to see the band. Barbara said I should have treated her the way Johnny treats Jessica. She said the band coming first was getting too painful. It's not like I was fooling around with some other girl! I miss her, but I can't be any different from what I am. So I don't have Johnny's "enormous capacity for feeling," so what?

"I've got to get to work."

"Okay." She's stuffing the towel back in her bag and zipping it up. "See you later."

"See you." I walk toward the school. The side door is the one that's unlocked. I can feel the sun burning the dew off the grass. It's going to be a scorcher.

I walk past the broad, empty front steps and I swear

I see the ghosts of kids yelling to their friends, tossing Frisbees, kidding around, having chicken fights, laughing. Years and years of kids have gone down these steps, rushing to someplace. I wish my turn hadn't come so soon. Real life, no more fun and games. Maybe Jessica's right about me. Maybe I'm too low on courage. Maybe one summer's too soon to settle for the lockstep.

I glance back at her over my shoulder. She's jogging around the track again. Interesting chick. If everything's going so great for her, why does she have to keep running in circles to feel free?

Tom

Going into a restaurant with Johnny's family is something else. We're at Nino's Wharf, overlooking Manhasset Bay. It's the best seafood place on the North Shore. Anybody else that comes in, they sit down at a table and that's it. We come in and the headwaiter's bowing and scraping to Johnny's father. It takes time to get everyone seated 'cause there's eleven of us: me, Jessica, Johnny, Johnny's father, Laurel, grandparents, two uncles, an aunt and a cousin, everybody that came out for Johnny's graduation from Bartholomew's. They pull two tables together, we have to get tables with a view of the sailboats, there's a lot of noise, the owner comes out to greet Johnny's father, we take over the whole room. Man, this family's big time wherever they go. It's like Johnny's father owns the place.

I'm glad it's air-conditioned. Bartholomew's auditorium wasn't and I was sweating like a pig. I never wear synthetics, I have to wear cotton, and even so, my shirt was soaking under my jacket. I can feel where the talcum is pilling in the creases. Sweating like that makes me feel ashamed. I worry about stains coming through the jacket.

Jessica's dressed, too, in high heels and a skirt. She looks radiant. Graduations at Bartholomew's are more formal than at North Bay. Johnny, obviously, didn't get any awards, but they're all happy as larks that he got the damn diploma. Bartholomew's must have spoon-fed him to get him through. There was one year I know he drank his lunch; his afternoon classes must have been a joke.

"Tom, what are you drinking?" Johnny's father says and he's ordering martinis and sours and you-name-it, and no one's going to say anything about we're underage. Not when Johnny's father is in charge.

"Martini on the rocks," I say. Why not? I can celebrate with Johnny this one time. The truth is I love the sonofabitch, he looks so happy and I'm glad for him.

I like Johnny's father, too. The guy has a sense of humor, easy to talk to, and there's that aura of real power under it all, you can't help but respect him, diamond pinkie ring and all. He looks a lot like Johnny. Johnny would never wear jewelry, though, and his father wears this huge, tacky ring. But then Johnny doesn't give off that feeling of don't-cross-me that the old man sends out. I like him; I wouldn't want him to lean on me.

"It was a nice graduation, wasn't it?" Jessica's sitting next to me.

"There was one great moment at ours," I tell her.

"What was that?"

"Your leap off the bleachers. It was supreme style."

"Oh, that," Jessica laughs. "I got carried away."

Darren and I were in line, waiting to take the assigned seats for graduates, and the line was moving very slowly past the bleachers. As we passed under Jessica, she called out "Hey, Tom!" and she took a flying leap. She was four rows up, she took this beautiful flying leap and I caught her in my arms. She knew I'd catch her. It was the way Mike describes the slam-dancers at CBGB's; when someone dives off the stage, he trusts that someone's going to break his fall. So I caught Jessica and she hugged me and then hugged Darren next to me. "Congratulations, boy graduates!" It was *me* that she flew to, though. It was a beautiful moment, it was great and not just for the status of everybody seeing her do that. I kept feeling her warmth and smelling her perfume all through the ceremony. Darren got the stage band award. I knew he would. I couldn't help thinking, though, that if there were no Darren, it would have been me. Second best gets nothing. No one thought of that. Nobody. Jessica's leap was the high point.

Later, my dad went on about it. "That was a very pretty girl there, in your arms," he kept saying. Mom chimed in with "and she sure likes you a lot, jumping at you like that," and on and on, looking so happy. They're teasing me, real cute, like I'm keeping this big secret and having this hot affair with Jessica. Well, Darren got the stage band award and Johnny's got Jessica, and I'm everyone's good buddy, cheering them on with my shit-eating grin.

Jessica's drinking a champagne cocktail and the waiters are buzzing all around, too eager, serving everybody like crazy, like Johnny's father is some kind of king.

Johnny's the heir apparent. He's all set. He doesn't have to go to college. All he has to do is drive around servicing his father's video games and pinball machines and whatever the hell else there is. If he doesn't become a rock star first. They've got part-interests in all kinds of things—a roller rink, some bars, even a racehorse.

"You'll have the lobster, Tom?" Johnny's father says.

"Yeah, sure." They serve mammoth lobster here, drowning in melted butter, the best on the Island. And I'll have the baked potato with sour cream and chives, and the salad with Roquefort, and, and, and . . .

I'm going on a diet. I made up my mind at graduation. I am. No one knows me at Bard. I have the whole summer to lose weight and I'll start fresh. No more "Chubbsy-wubbsy." I'm going to rewrite my life like a novel. But not tonight, because they've got this special bread at Nino's Wharf, it's something like garlic bread but with their own secret herbs, and man, I could eat three loaves. And their dessert menu is something else.

The appetizers are being served, and wine, and everybody is toasting Johnny. I can't stand the way Jessica's looking at him, stars in her eyes, and all because he managed to scrape through to a high school diploma!

"We've got some beautiful ladies at this table, Johnny," his father is saying expansively. It's true. Laurel is fantastic looking. She's got a body that doesn't stop. Tonight, her hair is up, very elaborate, and she's wearing false eyelashes. She never says much.

I'm halfway through the lobster, trying to keep the butter from dripping down my chin. I'm getting too full. I ate too much of that bread and I had the oysters Rockefeller and most of Jessica's avocado and shrimp, because she didn't like it. I'm too full, but this lobster can't go to waste, man.

I'm noticing how much Johnny looks like his father, not only features but mannerisms, too. The way Johnny's father has his hand resting on Laurel's shoulder, it becomes a display of possession. It's like he's claiming his property, the way he would put his hand firmly on the flank of his racehorse. And Johnny's got his hand on Jessica's shoulder exactly the same way! I can't stand to see it! Not on Jessica!

Now we're ordering from the dessert menu and it's a toss-up between the chocolate mousse and the pecan pie.

"The pecan pie with whipped cream," I finally tell the waiter.

Jessica's left to go to the ladies' room with the aunt and Johnny leans across her empty chair toward me.

"What's everybody doing tonight?"

"Hanging out at Darren's, I guess," I say.

"Jess and me are going to have to stay with the family for a while. We'll probably go over later."

Jess and me. He makes it sound exclusive.

"Yeah, maybe I'll see you there," I say.

I haven't seen Johnny so up in a long time. "My grandma's thrilled with Jessica." He laughs. " 'A nice girl,' she goes. 'Maybe you settle down, Johnny.' And you know something? Maybe I will."

I can't stand the way he's smiling. The bastard's got everything, just like it was coming to him, without even trying, and he had to go and take Jessica, too. I don't know what I'm going to say, though, until the words are out of my mouth.

"Just between us, Johnny," I say, "just because you're my best friend—you better keep your eye on Darren."

I take a certain satisfaction in watching the smile fade.

"What?" he says.

"I was going by the field this morning," I say. "Darren and Jessica were there. Like they were so deep into something, man, they didn't even see me go by."

"What're you saying?"

I feel paralyzed, watching my words float free-form above the table, independent of me. "Nothing," I say. "Just watch it."

"Tell me what—"

Jessica has come back to the table. The desserts are being served. Johnny motions to the waiter to bring him a brandy. Something's happening in his face. There's a muscle twitching at the side of his cheek and I swear his color's changed. Shit, I didn't know he cared that much about her. I suddenly feel fear like a cramp in my stomach.

Hell, I didn't say anything. I smooth the whipped cream down over the sides of the pie. Everything I said was true. I went by the field and I saw Darren and Jessica sitting on the bleachers. They were in the middle of some heavy conversation and they didn't see me. I was way off on the side and in a hurry to get home, so I never stopped to say hello. That's all. That's all I said.

Daylight is fading and the picture window frames a red sunset over Manhasset Bay, a scarlet background for the white sails, too colorful to be real.

Jessica, next to me, is talking, animated and sparkling.

I don't want to see Johnny's face. I've known him forever—I love the guy. Hell, I didn't really say anything. Nothing to it. I hunch over the table and dig into the pie.

Mike

There must be a full moon out tonight. I'd go out to check, just to see if the connection between full moon and insanity actually holds, but it's not worth the hassle. We're at the Three Deuces and I don't want to go anyplace near the door. I have this badly doctored driver's license for an ID and there's a new guy at the door, checking.

"I'm playing in the band here in a couple of weeks," I told him. "What are you bothering me for?"

He checked me, anyway. Jessica has a beautiful ID that Johnny got for her, so she doesn't have to worry anymore. She used to have a very original way of getting in. She'd go down the alley where the girls' bathroom window is, open it, and climb through. She'd land on the sink, hands first, and startle the hell out of any broad washing up in there, but she never had to go through the ID check. Tom and Darren have official cards from Tempo University, complete with photos. The owner and the regular bouncer know us. It's just this new guy at the door that's taking himself too seriously.

Darren wants us to watch the band that's playing tonight. He's getting to be a very nervous dude. I mean, we've actually seen bands before. But he's got all this excess energy, worrying about this Ryan thing coming up. He's going around telling us to watch tonight's band, see what they do, et cetera, et cetera. All they do is Grateful Dead cover numbers and they've brought their own claque with them, a bunch of kids I've never seen around here before. It's like a time warp back to the sixties. They're wearing the Indian skirts, shirts and beads, waving their arms, doing these disconnected dances. Peace and love is their shtick. We're entering the twilight zone. The drummer is good, though.

We're all here—Johnny at the bar, Tom at a table with some kids from North Bay, Jessica dancing around and having fun, me and Darren talking.

"You know what they did?" Darren is saying. "They chartered a bus. It's outside in the parking lot. That's something to remember when we play out of town. You bring in your own following, charge so much a head for the bus, and you look good, with this big friggin' following."

"Don't worry, when we play, all of North Bay will be here," I say. "We'll look good."

"I know, I know," Darren says, "but spread the word anyway. July 23. Tell everybody. Saturday, July 23."

Then he goes over to talk to Tom. I'll lay odds he's asking Tom to check out chartered buses in case we get a gig out of town.

I join Johnny at the bar. He's tossing down margaritas, almost like the old days, and watching Jessica. She's dancing by herself in a parody of the stoned, freak style and shoots a big grin over to us. The band is playing "U.S. Blues" and messing it up bad, but nobody seems to notice.

Darren comes over after awhile and he's in a good mood, probably because we're so much better than these jokers. He even gives Johnny a playful punch on the shoulder. That's high spirits for Darren.

"Johnny," he says. "How's it going?"

"Great," Johnny says. "Couldn't be better." He's slowly licking the salt off the rim of his glass and then he laughs this weird laugh. "I had a dream about you, Darren. Man, it was so funny. I dreamed I killed you. It was the funniest thing, man."

Darren takes his hand off Johnny's shoulder, quick, and looks at me.

I shrug. "Full moon tonight."

Darren moves off.

Tom's still at the table, trying to move in on a little blond fox and she's trying to edge away. The band is playing "Truckin' " like the inept clones they are and even the drummer doesn't sound good anymore. Johnny's watching Jessica through the smoke and Jessica's oblivious of him, dancing in circles with the Grateful Deadheads, having a good time. It's a zoo.

The music stops and Jessica's on her way back to us. Some old guy at the end of the bar pulls her arm as she passes and says something. She looks annoyed for a moment and then keeps going. Johnny's over there like a shot and leads her back to our end.

"What did he say to you?"

"Nothing."

"Damn it, I want to know!"

"For God's sake, Johnny—"

"I want to know what he said!"

"It doesn't matter!"

"You tell me what he said and he's going to apologize or I'll ram his teeth down his throat!"

"No! Just because some stupid jerk—"

"How many times do I have to tell you! In a public place, you stay at my side!"

"I was just dancing—"

"What did he say to you?"

"Nothing! It's over! It doesn't matter!"

"Play nice, kiddies," I say to them. They don't react and I go back to sipping my beer. I'm the only sane bystander in the place.

"You're supposed to stay right by my side! I don't want you to move!"

"Johnny, that's crazy."

"I can't leave you alone for a minute. There's always someone! Some guy at a bar, some guy on the street—"

"Look, I can't help it if some idiot talks to me. It's not my fault!"

"And you and Darren—"

"What? What? What about Darren?"

"I know all about it. I know about you and Darren."

"Johnny, please. Don't get weird, Johnny. . . ."

The music begins, but Jessica doesn't dance again. She and Johnny are hunched over the bar, arguing. Johnny's face is white and Jessica is biting her lip.

It's a strange night. Bad vibrations.

Johnny

I'm not going to say anything tonight. I'm just going to stay here in the kitchen for a while and have a quiet drink. Then I'll go back out to Jess and not say anything, like nothing's happened.

We're playing at this girl's sweet sixteen party. There's a keg out in the backyard and the band was up on the patio. The sound system wasn't that good, but nobody cared. Jessica was terrific in the first set, relaxed and into it, and looking great. The kids were yelling and cheering, and I was going all the way with "Out of Control" and trying out the new song Darren cowrote with Mike, "Botulism in Mom's Apple Pie." It went over great. By the time we got our break, I was flying high, sweating and feeling good, feeling this was going to be one of our good nights.

There's a big buffet set up near the pool. We're helping ourselves there and at the keg, and everyone in the band is way up.

"If it goes like this the night Ryan sees us . . . ," Mike is saying.

The girl's parents said to help ourselves. They don't know what they're in for with Tom. I'm kind of laughing to myself, watching him demolish the sliced turkey platter. Then I notice Jessica is off to the side with some dude. I go over and bring her a beer.

"Oh, Johnny, thanks," she says, bright-eyed. "This is Mark Evers, he was in my Math 11 class."

Well, okay, so she wants to say hello to a kid in her class, but they go on talking and talking. They're saying stuff like "Remember when the Mathletes," and kidding around about cotangents and Pythagorean theorem. Jessica's laughing hard. What the hell could be so funny about R squared? I stand there. They're busy talking and I'm getting pissed off. I feel stupid, rooted there, waiting for her to get through. Who is this guy, anyway? I'm not going to blow up this time, so I go through the mob of kids, inside, into the kitchen.

The air-conditioning hits me. There's bottles of soda lined up on a shiny black counter and a tray of leftover hors d'oeuvres. There's a garbage can overflowing with paper plates. The maid is loading the dishwasher and there's a couple off in the corner, near the fridge, whispering.

This cute ponytailed chick in a flippy pink miniskirt follows me in.

"You were so great," she's squealing. "I love the way you sing. Oh, you were so great!"

She's cute, all right, with full lips the same pink as the skirt, and for a minute, I'm almost tempted. But the truth is, I don't want the old days back. So I'm quietly drinking my beer and thinking as she rattles on.

"You know something? The neighbors on both sides called up because of you guys, but Tammy's mother was so great, she said . . . on a Saturday night . . . I mean, too much . . ." Giggle, giggle. "My name's Sandy and . . ." Giggle. "I love your band. I love the way you all move. . . ."

I nod every once in awhile. I'm going to calm down and then go back out to Jessica. We've been fighting too much and she gets upset. I'm not going to let myself spoil things tonight.

"You don't talk much, do you?" Sandy goes.

"I save my voice for singing," I tell her, "so let's skip the preliminaries, baby."

She hesitates and for a minute there, I'm worried she's going to agree to skip the preliminaries. But then she shrugs and leaves. She's got a cute little ass twitching out the door. I'm almost tempted but—I love Jessica.

I didn't know it could be like this. I didn't know you could be best friends and have sex, too. That's some combination. One night, we were following our tradition of having pizza in bed afterward and talking, feeling so close, and Jessica opened up to me. She said I've taught her to be spontaneous. She said I'm good for her. She was telling me how her brother Larry used to be the big attraction in her family and how she was always an also-ran. Nothing she could do—the guitar or getting good marks—could come close to Larry's hockey glory. She was lonely inside her iceberg family; she used to call her mother the Snow Queen and her father the Vanishing Man. She and her mom are getting along better now and that's good. I never felt so tender to anyone. I want to be good for her. I could kill anyone that hurts her feelings.

I found myself telling her about the dyslexia and, saying it out loud, it didn't even seem that bad. She knows I'm naturally smart and she can understand why I hated school so much. And then I found myself talking to her about the one thing I'd never talk to anyone about, not even Tom. I talked about my mother. I mean, my dad's a great guy, but he has his faults and I can see why she objected to his fooling around. I can understand her leaving. What I can't understand is the way she took off for Florida without me. I like my dad, we get along fine—but her leaving me behind like that . . . I was only in fifth grade when she left me. She has to be some evil bitch. And I told Jess about all that.

I didn't know it was possible to feel so close to someone. And no matter what, I'm not going to spoil it with Jessica. I'm not going to let myself get mad if she forgets about me for a little while and wants to talk about cotangents.

"Hey, Johnny. What're you doing?" It's Tom.

"Just cooling off," I say. "I'll be out in a minute."

"Darren was looking for you. He says the next time we do 'Apple Pie,' we'll do that chorus very, very slow and kind of fade out on 'This apple's got a worm.' Kind of an eerie effect."

"Sounds good."

"Listen, Johnny," Tom says. "About Darren. You know what I said the other day? At Nino's Wharf?"

"Yeah."

"Look, I don't think he's really after Jessica."

Two guys brush past us on their way to the fridge. They're making a racket, getting some ice out.

"Darren and me had a talk about that," I say. "He swore up and down his only interest in Jessica is for the band. Period."

"Right, Johnny," Tom says. "That's what I think." I'm wondering why he looks so relieved. I guess because he's a real friend; he's glad things are okay between me and Jessica.

"I don't know about believing Darren or not," I say. "I believe Jessica. You can't begin to imagine what she's like. She's so beautiful. . . ."

He turns his face away from me, but not before I see his sad, defeated expression. Tom ought to have somebody, too.

"Hey, Tom," I say. "There's a cute pink miniskirt wandering around looking for action." I'm steering him out the door.

"Forget it," he says.

"No kidding. She likes the band. She likes the way we move."

"Lay off, Johnny."

"Come on, I'll set it up for you." We're out of the kitchen and walking along the slate path, past a bunch of Japanese lanterns. I'm looking around for Sandy.

"Damn it, I said lay off!"

I put my arm around Tom's shoulder, just kidding around. "What's the matter, baby, you don't like girls?"

He pushes my arm off violently and I'm kind of surprised. I guess he gets defensive on account of he's shy with broads.

"Okay," I say, "but I hate to see her talent going to waste." I'm walking ahead of him on the path, toward the patio.

"You're so damn sure of yourself," he hisses behind me. "Did you ever think Darren and Jessica are telling you this only-good-friends crap just to keep the lid on? Until after the Three Deuces? Until after July 23? Ever think of that, Johnny?"

I whirl around. Tom is in the shadows. He goes off into the crowd.

There's a pulse in the back of my head that starts pounding. There's a harsh buzzing sound and then I realize I'm standing next to one of those blue-light electric bug killers. There's a buzz every few seconds as another bug bites the dust.

Darren and Jessica? That's just like Darren. He'd swear to anything to hold the band together until Ryan sees us.

Some girls cross in front of me and then one of them turns around and doubles back. This one is chubby, with tight blond ringlets.

"Aren't you the singer?" she says.

My head is pounding and the damn blue light keeps buzzing.

"You're so cute. The way you sing that song"—giggle—"the one with smoking grass and saying, you know," giggle . . .

I stare at her blankly until she goes away.

Darren! No one noticed Jessica until I picked her out. And then, all of a sudden, everyone's looking her over. If I've got something, everyone figures it's the best and everyone else wants some. So now Darren's moving in and he can write those damn lyrics and poems for her, too!

I'm heading for the keg. Damn it, all they've got here is beer!

The truth is, Jessica's been doing good in front of the band and I hate the way everyone looks at her. I try to keep those feelings down, but I don't like her being public like that.

And now Darren! The little bitch!

There's a mob around the keg and I'm elbowing my

way through. If I can find Mike, I'll hit him for a joint.

"Johnny." It's Jessica. "Where did you go?"

I take a deep breath. I'm not going to say anything. "I was in the kitchen. To cool off."

"I was looking for you."

"Yeah, well, you were busy with your cotangent buddy."

"We were in Mathletes together. So many funny things happened when—"

"Yeah, that Pytha-friggin'-whatsis theory's a laugh riot."

I see her face going tight and I take a deep breath. I'm not going to fight with her. I'm not going to spoil things.

"The band did great, huh?" I finally say, with effort.

"I think so," she goes, politely. "It's all coming together, I think."

"It seems to be," I say.

What am I doing, making small talk with Jessica!

"Come on," I say, "let's get out of here."

"We can't. We're on again in a couple of minutes."

"Oh, shit."

"Why? What's the matter, Johnny?"

"This party sucks."

"We can leave right after—"

Darren passes by, carrying a handful of pretzels. He pops a pretzel in Jessica's mouth as he goes by. I'm enraged. Where does he get off, putting anything in Jessica's mouth!

Jessica's still talking about the band, talking around the pretzel. I don't know what the hell she's saying.

"Where were you this morning?" I say.

"What?"

Keep your cool, I tell myself. Don't say word one.

"I called your house at nine this morning," I say. "Where were you?"

She looks puzzled. "I told you. I'm getting back to running."

"Nobody runs that long. You weren't home at ten either because I called again at ten. Your mother said you weren't home yet."

"So?"

"So where were you?"

"I told you. At the track."

"Right. At the track. Doing what at the track?"

"Johnny, come on. Don't start."

Chill out, I tell myself. I keep my voice low. "No. Just answer me. What were you doing?"

"What do you think I was doing? I ran for a while and then I sat on the bleachers and talked to Darren for a while and. . . ." She sounds nervous.

"You arranged to meet Darren, right?"

"Johnny, this is so crazy! I told you the other night. I sit and rest and have some juice before I walk home. Darren doesn't start work until ten, but the only time he can get a ride to the high school is nine-thirty, because that's when his mother goes to work. Okay so far?" She's talking real slow, with make-believe patience, like one of those bitchy elementary school teachers. "So he gets there early and has coffee. We talk for a few minutes and then he goes to work and I walk home. Sometimes we talk about the band. Sometimes we talk about people we know. Maybe sometime we'll talk about the weather! And I don't know why I'm telling you this again."

"Yeah," I say. I take a deep breath for the clincher.

"Yeah, but why do you run at *just that time*?" I've yelled the last three words into her face.

"Because that's when it's cool! It's cool in the morning! I run when it's cool! I run in the mornings!" She's shouting and we've collected an audience. I see Tom's face in the crowd.

Just before she turns and storms away, I think I see tears welling up in Jessica's eyes.

I've done it again. I tried not to, but it got away from me again. I've spoiled it again.

Jessica

I come in through the kitchen and the screen door bangs shut behind me. My sweatband and my T-shirt are soaking wet and all I want is quarts and quarts of cold water. My little can of orange juice wasn't enough this morning.

"Jessica, is that you?" Mom's voice.

"No, it's your friendly neighborhood burglar." My standard witticism. There's been a rash of burglaries around North Bay and a lot of them turn out to be skinny junior high kids with habits to support.

It was too hot to run this morning. It's the third day in a row over ninety. I woke up early this morning, nervous about performing at the Three Deuces tonight for that man, Ryan. And I was depressed about Johnny. So I went out to the track. But it was too hot and I didn't get enough running in to unwind.

"I'll be right down, Jessica," Mom calls.

"Okay."

I gulp some ice water. My shorts are sticking to me. I'm longing for Johnny's air-conditioned house and Johnny's pool and splashing under Johnny's waterfall, and that's exactly what I shouldn't be concentrating on. Because, air-conditioning aside, everything is wrong between me and Johnny.

Monday, when we had dinner at the Sea Haven, he said someone at the next table was making eyes at me. He said I encouraged it. Then, last night at rehearsal, he said Darren was standing too close to me. He said Tom noticed it, too. He kept talking about it all the way home.

Finally, I screamed at him. "Yes! Yes! Yes, Darren's good looking! Yes! Now leave me alone!"

I went to sleep feeling burdened and I woke up the same way. I care about Johnny, but I don't think I can take much more of this.

Mom comes into the kitchen. "Johnny stopped by while you were out."

"This early?" He usually goes out with the guys after he drops me off and then sleeps until noon. Unless he has to work for his father.

"I was so embarrassed when I answered the door," Mom says. "I was in my bathrobe and I didn't have a speck of makeup on."

There's a coy quality that makes me look at her.

"He brought roses again, *and* a box of chocolates. He wanted to surprise you; he was so cute about it. He had to fill the vase and set it up in your room himself. It was really so cute. And then I said, 'You're very sweet to her,' you know, just to give him a compliment. Well, he said,

'I know, but she doesn't appreciate it.' Jessica, he had the saddest look on his face. You have to be more appreciative of . . ."

I can picture his sad look. He gets very dramatic.

"He said he was doing some errands, but he'd be home by eleven. He wants you to call him, so be sure to—"

"Okay."

"Be sure to call him. I don't want him to think I didn't give you the message."

"Don't worry. He won't take it as a personal attack."

"I don't understand you. Most girls would give anything to . . . You don't know how lucky you . . . Sometimes I wish . . . He's so loving, Jessica and . . . take it from me, love like that doesn't grow on trees and . . ."

She goes on and I escape to my room.

There are two deep red buds, nestled against the ferns. The card is propped against the vase. "All my love, always, forever." It's not the words, it's his childlike print that touches me. I do feel love for him. That's what makes me so confused.

Automatically, I flip the corner of my quilt back. Right, another card on my sheet. "Love you again." I think if I find another card somewhere, I'll go berserk. Maybe I really am an ungrateful monster.

There might even be a little truth in Johnny's craziness. Maybe having Johnny's stamp of approval has made other guys more interested in me. Sometimes I feel Mike looking me over curiously, checking out what Johnny sees in me. Maybe being loved has changed me into someone warmer and more womanly. Maybe girls who are loved have a subtly altered body language. There might be a germ of truth in it, but with Johnny everything gets wildly exaggerated. Exaggerated and unreasonable.

There was the night he told me about his mother. I was very sympathetic at first. He sat hunched over the coffee table, a wounded look on his face. I was trying to comfort him. "You're mad because she left you, but look at it this way. If your dad had left, wouldn't you feel abandoned by him? And mad at him?"

"I want to live with my dad," he said. "We get along great. Why should I be mad at him?"

I tried again. "I know. All I'm saying is you can't have it both ways. You can't live with your mother *and* your dad, so—"

"But I want it both ways!" he said, furious at me. "You don't understand!"

"Okay," I said. "Forget it. Don't let reason interfere with your feelings."

"You *would* take her side!" He slammed an ashtray on the table. It made a sound like a shot and shattered.

A piece of glass hit my arm and cut me. It was just a little cut, a drop of blood. I was too shocked to move. Johnny felt terrible. He wiped the blood. He checked for slivers of glass. He got a Band-Aid that I didn't want.

"God, I'm sorry, Jess. I don't know what happened. I'm sorry. I get too emotional, you know, about my mother."

Okay, so Johnny overreacts. Why should that give me such an anxious, creepy feeling?

I don't want to think about it. I'm hot and clammy. I kick my sneakers off—there's a new blister—and stretch out on the bed. I'm supposed to save my energy for to-night. I wonder if Ryan will really show up. I keep hear-ing Tom and Mike talking about groups going on the road, building up a following, demos and tapes and videos, all this stuff as if they know something about it. As if we're more than a bunch of kids practicing in a basement. I don't want to think about that, either. It's making me too nervous.

The fragrance of roses permeates the room, much stronger than I'd expect from two flowers. Dead roses from earlier in the week are still in my wastepaper basket. The "I love you this much" pillow is propped up on my bed. If I turn my head, I'll see the jewelry box on my dresser. It contains the little diamond stud earrings Johnny gave me after our fight at that girl's sweet sixteen party. Mementos of him are everywhere. Johnny has even invaded my room.

Jessica

We're all riding in the van with the equipment, Johnny driving, and we're getting psyched up. Dale's brother Jimmy is going to mix the sound and he's in the car behind us with some other guys.

"Look at that, will you?" Mike says. "We've got our own friggin' *entourage*!"

"We are a hot band, man," Tom is yelling. "We are a damn hot band!"

Johnny stops for a light at the corner of Lloyd Hill and the Boulevard. There's a group of girls in front of the pizzeria.

"Hey, beautiful!" he yells. They all look up. "Come on over to Three Deuces! Hey, come on!"

"We can't," one of them calls back. "We don't have proof."

"That's okay." The light changes and the van is moving on. "Tell them you're with the band. Out of Control, okay?"

I can see them looking after the van until we turn the next corner.

"The master's voice," Mike says. "I bet you anything they come."

Everyone's loud and hyper. Everyone but Darren. He's drawn into himself. We slow down in traffic on Shore Road and there's a guy in the car next to us picking his nose. We're all laughing uproariously as Mike does an exaggerated imitation, but he never notices us.

By the time we get to Three Deuces, we're very up and then we have to wait around for the sound to get set up. The long waits are the hardest. A few people straggle in. It's early for the Three Deuces crowd. Waiting makes Johnny jumpy. The time goes.

Darren tests the mikes. "Okay," he says. "Ready for a sound check?"

Jimmy's at the mixing board. "Whenever."

We halfheartedly go through "Now" while Jimmy makes adjustments. We're all saving energy. Finally, "Okay, that's it."

More people come in. I go into the ladies' room to check my makeup; the Three Deuces has no backstage. I put some more gloss over my lips because I've chewed it all off. I look up at the window over the sink where I used to sneak in. Another world. I'm wearing a green satin minidress, cut very low, and I feel detached from myself.

Annie bursts in through the swinging door. "Darren

said to tell you. Dennis Ryan just walked in. Come on out."

"Oh," I say. I feel my stomach contract.

"Don't worry, you're terrific. You look great."

"Just *mah*velous, dahling," I say.

We leave the ladies' room. The Three Deuces is filling up. It looks like a lot of North Bay High is here. I guess we spread the word pretty well.

Tom, Mike, Darren, and Johnny are talking to two guys at a table. The one in the suit is Ryan; he's younger than I expected. The other one has something to do with A&R. Ryan does most of the talking—about how he managed Thin Ice, built them up way back when, about how he likes coming back to North Bay, he used to live in the white house on Cove Road, about all the publicity his other group's tour is getting. We're all busy impressing each other. I'm smiling a lot. He's saying something about "the bottom line is" while his eyes check out my cleavage. I don't like him. Then it's almost time to go on and we head toward the kitchen, to get ourselves ready.

The tables are filling and the bar is crowded, with people standing. As we walk by, we're getting thumbs-up signs. We've got a following, we really do!

We stand close together in the kitchen. We don't dress in any uniform way. Darren and Mike are in T-shirts and jeans, Mike is loaded down with chains, Tom is in leather trying to look like a Hell's Angel instead of a fat, suburban kid, Johnny is in an immaculate white shirt and perfectly tailored gray pants, and I'm wearing what he calls my "seduction special."

"Linda Ann Garcia and Thin Ice started in North Bay," Mike says, "and look where they are now." Mike looks very young to me tonight, in spite of the mohawk and the chains. I can see him as a ten-year-old waiting for Christmas.

"Can lightning strike twice in the same place?" Darren mutters through tight, frozen lips.

I feel unreal. I am numb.

Time is either running very slow or very fast. It's been rackingly slow since we first came here, waiting, hanging around, and now it's speeded up insanely and we'll be catapulted on in a second!

"Come on, come on, come on, let's go!" Johnny is coiled tight as a spring.

We do our good-luck routine. There's no kidding around; it's a solemn ritual. Everyone hugs everyone. It's important not to miss anyone. I hug Mike, Tom, Darren, and then Johnny, last and longest. The guys hug each other. I love them all, right now, harder than I will ever love anyone else. We are a *band.* No one says a word.

There's a strong smell of stale onions in the kitchen. The dishwasher in his dirty white apron grins at us. He's missing a tooth. Then we rush through the door and the noise of the Three Deuces hits us and we're on!

Mike starts the beat and the first line of "Out of Control" draws an amazing roar from the crowd. Darren said to do part of the chorus for our signature and then go right into "Now." He didn't think "Out of Control" was right for Ryan, but the reaction is so big! Finally, Darren calls, "The whole thing! Keep going!" Mike laughs and Johnny is off and flying.

They're littering the shopping malls
They're humping on the floor

They're trampling suburban lawns
'Cause the good life is a bore
They are . . .
Out of control!
Rampant and amok!
Smokin' dope
And sayin'—!

We all come in on the chorus, we have one voice, we blend together and become one huge thing, intertwined. Johnny takes the rhythm with his body; Mike plays the melody on his drums; bass, guitar, and keyboards weave around and through each other; and the chant from the crowd becomes part of it, too. This is our down-home audience, all right, washing over us, loving us because we're one of them.

"Darren!" someone calls. "Darren!"

Then, a little later, another voice. "Hey, Mike!"

These are kids we know casually from around school, suddenly calling our names out, suddenly claiming us, reaching out for a piece of our one-night celebrity.

Big raucous cheer at the end of "Out of Control." Then "Now," "Queen of Burger King," a lot of people dancing . . .

I tried the new solo and it worked! I never felt freer! And Johnny is pulling everything together, hammering at the lyrics, working himself into a frenzy, and then "Bag Lady Blues" . . .

Scavenger lady's
Got a hunger Gucci cannot ease
Bag-dragging lady . . .

Johnny bends the word "hunger" into a howl of desolation that sends a chill up my back. Under the lights, Johnny's skin looks dead-white, his hair as black as a raven's wing. He seems consumed with emotion, even on "Moral Majority." Even if the lyrics mean nothing to him, he sings them with white-hot intensity. He whips his head around and the light catches a stream of sweat from his forehead.

Then "Sweet Love Gone Sour" and he is mesmerizing. It's all Johnny. There's something coming through that goes far beyond the words. Johnny puts no limits on, he's a high-wire act, a hairbreadth from careening into thin air, scary and exhilarating, a touch of insanity that makes the audience roar.

Then it's over. Darren takes the mike. "Thank you, you're wonderful, don't go 'way, thank you, stick around for more" and the first set is over. He sounds happy. I knew it. I knew we were good!

We go down to the bar. Arms are reaching for us and kids I hardly know are clutching at me, saying "Jessica!" I see the blond woman from long ago in Darren's basement streak toward Johnny, throw her arms around him and give him a long kiss on the mouth. Ryan shakes hands with everyone, says nice things, smiles, and leaves. He hasn't said anything definite.

"He likes us," Darren says. "He'll call me later."

Then I'm gulping down a large Coke and Johnny is licking the salt from his margarita.

"I'm sorry about that, Jess," he says.

"Sorry about what?" My mouth was so dry. It always gets dry when I'm nervous.

"Marlene. I couldn't help it, she came over to me and—"

"You mean the blond? I don't care, Johnny. Don't worry about it." He is sweetly old-fashioned in his effort to be true to me.

"How do you mean, you don't care?"

"It's all right. It doesn't bother me."

"It doesn't bother you?"

"No."

"I can't understand you!" he explodes. "If you loved me, you'd be jealous!"

I look at his expression and I think, not again, not now. I try to smile him out of it. "Why should I be jealous? I'm sorry for her. I have you and she doesn't, right?"

I've said the right thing. He smiles back, satisfied.

The second set is almost as high as the first. Some people have left, but more have come in and the roomful of bodies is bouncing to "Bedrock Beat." Then they yell for Johnny to sing "Out of Control" again. This is a love-in. This is home. I wonder if it felt like this to Thin Ice when they came back to play the Nassau Coliseum. The big difference, of course, is that we're not coming back home—we haven't left yet.

The set ends and I order another large Coke at the bar, with lots of ice. Johnny is surrounded at the other end of the room, animated, jumping. I'm full of relief at all the things that didn't happen. I didn't break a string, the amplifier didn't go out, I didn't forget—

"Jessica?"

"My God! Bobby! How are you?" An old friend of my

brother's. I used to have a crush on him. I used to daydream about his blue eyes.

"I didn't know you were with this group. Some surprise! And you're good!"

"Thanks. How are you, anyway?"

"Okay, great. How's Larry doing? Haven't seen him around at all. . . ."

"He's staying with his roommate in Boston. He's not coming home till the end of August."

"Say hello for me, okay?"

"Sure."

"Boy, I can't believe Larry's bratty little kid sister, all grown up and gorgeous. You know something, I ought to take you out sometime."

"I've got a boyfriend," I say. I feel a twinge of regret. Bobby was always my favorite of all the guys on the hockey team.

"Oh, hell. Bad timing, huh?" He grins at me sheepishly.

"I'll take a rain check on it," I say. "I'll call you when we break up."

"You've got to," he says. "You've got to save my ego, Jessie."

We're kidding, of course. I think I was kidding. I don't know what made me say that, anyway. I don't think of Bobby that way anymore.

By the fourth and last set, we've all run down. All except Johnny. He's giving and giving, more and more, from some endless reservoir. Johnny makes the crowd wild, everybody wants a piece of Johnny, everybody wants to tap into him. Darren's lyrics, Mike's drumbeats,

Tom and me at our best, are background. He's burning, burning, reaching deeper and higher for more. More sensation, more euphoria, more love, more adulation. More. More than I can handle. I can still hear the echo of my voice: ". . . when we break up. . . ."

Jerry

I don't know what happens. Things fall apart right in front of my eyes, just when I think they're going good. It's like I've reached for a candy bar—an Almond Joy—and I'm getting ready for that sweet coconut taste and all of a sudden, some joker's put a time bomb in it. That's the way I feel—blown apart, with bones shattered, bits of flesh clinging to the walls. And I don't even know what happened.

We left the Three Deuces after three. I was soaking wet, still feeling great, holding on to that high. The way Ryan shook my hand, I could tell he thought I was good. We brought the equipment back to Darren's and a whole bunch of people crowded in. Great night. Everybody was happy and Jessica was saying all this stuff to me. "I was so proud of you. You were fantastic!" Things like that. I was thinking I want to do this every night, for real. I didn't even really come down. I had that drained, relaxed feeling you get after a good night.

Later, driving her home, I remembered about the guy she was talking to at the bar. I asked her who he was and she said her brother's friend from hockey. I mentioned that she was talking to him for too long a time, but in a casual way. All I said was, "Why can't you be more like Laurel?" I wasn't yelling at her or anything.

"Like Laurel? You want me to be more like Laurel?" I never expected her to flare up like that for no reason.

"Well, Laurel's happy to wait for my dad to come home. She's always there. She won't go and talk to a million guys or—"

"Or do anything. She's always there!"

"Well, yeah, she's satisfied to stay at my dad's side, like in a public place and—"

"Laurel is stoned all the time! She's on ludes all the time! You told me that yourself. She's unconscious and waiting for your dad! Is that what you want?" Jessica is really mad. She's yelling at me.

"I don't mean exactly that, but—" I start to say. She won't let me finish.

"Does your dad time how long she talks to somebody? What's the limit? Two minutes? Five minutes? Did I pass the five-minute mark with Bobby?"

I don't like it when she gets sarcastic with me. It makes me feel bad.

"I just mentioned it," I go. I don't understand her. She ought to be happy that I watch out for her all the time, in public places or anyplace. "Look, Laurel knows how to act. You're too immature, Jess, and you don't know enough to appreciate—"

I'm trying to explain to her. She's still very young and I'm not mad. She's quiet for a long time and I think maybe she's taking it to heart. So I go on. "You act too friendly. You don't understand how guys think. Like, that jerk was looking down your dress the whole time. Even with Mike, you—"

Then she says, in a funny voice, "Pull over someplace."

"What for?"

"I have to tell you something."

What does she want to tell me that I have to pull over for? We're on Main Street and I park at the curb.

"I'll always love you, in a way," she goes. "I've never felt closer to anyone, but—"

I'm beginning to get a feeling like the Almond Joy is about to blow up.

"I'm not mad at you," I say, fast. "It's okay about that guy."

She goes right on. "I guess I'm not ready for . . . I feel guilty all the time and . . . not really happy . . . I think we should cool it for a while and . . ."

Main Street is all closed down. Hardly any cars going by. We're parked in front of the deli and it's all locked up.

". . . always be friends and . . . not spoil the good memories . . ."

"No!" I shout. "No! I don't want this!"

"It can't work out if . . . one person . . . more than the other . . ."

"What are you talking about?" I go. "What the hell are you talking about?"

". . . instead of going out . . . if we see each other sometimes . . . good friends and . . ."

"Don't do this to me, Jessica!"

She talks in circles, a lot of words. I watch a car's headlights coming out of the post office driveway. The traffic light on the corner flashes on and off. Green. Red. Green. Go. Walk. Don't. Stop. Jessica! Stop!

Jessica

The words come tumbling out, familiar but somewhat out of order. I have a sense of déjà vu. Have I rehearsed it all in my mind before, not knowing I was going to say it? Or maybe I've dreamed this, complete with the flashing traffic light and the dim sausage shapes hanging in the delicatessen window.

He's not looking at me. He's staring straight ahead, through the windshield. He has the stony, stubborn look of a child refusing to listen.

"You did everything right," I say. "It's not you. It's me." I almost believe that. There's so much about Johnny that's lovable.

I wish he would say something.

"Maybe you're right. Maybe I am too immature. I feel hemmed in, Johnny. I can't help it." I want to cry.

I see flashes of scenes: Johnny on water skis, his body moving in perfect harmony, silhouetted against a cloudless sky. Johnny laughing with wholehearted innocence at the "Tom and Jerry" cartoons. Johnny, polished and commanding with a headwaiter, with reservations, with a limo driver. So many parts of Johnny.

"I'm sorry," I say.

He won't look at me.

"I guess things went too far too fast and—" I say, "and I don't want to go out anymore."

I want to hold him again, but I can't. "We'll still see each other in the band and we'll be friends and—"

He could be so loving. "Maybe we can even get together again sometime, maybe I just need a breather. . . ."

He suddenly starts the car and pulls away from the curb with a squeal of tires. He drives furiously, too fast, and I'm glad we don't have far to go. He still doesn't look at me. I see that he's swallowing hard and I realize with a shock that he's fighting tears.

Johnny

I couldn't say a word to her. I dropped her off and drove home, like on automatic pilot. I can't believe this is happening. I can't handle it.

No one's home. They went up to Vermont yesterday. Jessica and me should have come right over here after the Three Deuces. We could have skinny-dipped in the pool and then made love and everything would have been good between us. It always is when we're by ourselves. We should have skipped Darren's. It's being around other people that spoiled everything.

I go to the bar and pour myself a shot of Dad's Glenfiddich. It burns going down. He's been saying things about my drinking too much of his scotch. The trick is to finish the whole bottle. If I leave one half-empty, he'll notice.

I just left her a little while ago and I miss her so much already.

I go for the phone. She answers and her voice is sleepy.

"Jess," I tell her, "when it's us, by ourselves, it's good. You know it is."

"No," she goes. "It's not."

"But I love you," I tell her.

"I know," she says. There's a long pause. "I'm sorry, I'm half-asleep. I can't even think now."

"I want to talk to you."

"We can talk some more later," she mumbles.

"Jess, we've got a lot to talk about. You can't—"

"In the morning, okay?"

"Jess, I miss you!"

"Johnny. Oh, Johnny, good-night. Let me get back to sleep."

"Wait—" and she's hung up. I'm crying. I don't think she could know that over the phone.

I pour myself another shot and I take it over to the couch. The margaritas wore off a long time ago; it's like I'm starting from scratch. I lie down and look at the ceiling for a long time.

I get up and go into the kitchen. I rummage around the refrigerator. It's packed full of stuff and there's nothing I want to eat.

I can't be alone like this.

It's Sunday already. I was going to take her to dinner tonight. I was going to try that new place that just opened up. It's supposed to have a garden in the back, with candlelight and everything. She'll love it. She said herself, I did everything right. Everything would be great except for—except for—except for Darren! Man, how could I be so dumb! It's Darren! Just like Tom said, they were waiting until after the Three Deuces gig! I was so dumb! I let Darren move in on her!

I rush right over to the phone. She answers on the first ring.

"Jessica, listen—"

"Do you know the time? You can't call now! You'll wake my father and—"

"Jessica, listen. It's that snake Darren, right?"

"You woke me up and—"

"The snake in the grass. Listen, he's not going to love you the way I do. No one's ever going to love you the way I do. I—"

"Johnny, didn't you hear anything I said? It has nothing to do with Darren."

"The hell it doesn't."

"This is crazy. Let me get back to sleep and—"

The bitch! She's going to hang up on me again! "You know what's wrong with you, Jessica? You got a split personality. You ought to see a friggin' shrink. You ought to—"

"Later, Johnny." I hear the click on the other end. I hurl the phone to the floor. It makes a little murmuring sound, like something alive.

She's got a split personality, that's the truth. One minute, she's like an angel from heaven, all sweet and soft. You can see the purity shining from her face. And then she turns sarcastic and evil, lying to me, fooling around with Darren. Queen Bitch.

Darren

For that whole first week after we played the Three Deuces, I jumped for the phone every time it rang. Especially at night. I figured Ryan for a night person.

I never knew we got so many asinine phone calls. Some whispery, giggly little girl who won't leave her name keeps calling for Frankie. Is he getting to that age already? Then some idiot from a market research service wants to talk to me about toothpaste. And there's a lot of people out there trying to sell newspaper subscriptions and Pocono vacation sites. A world of strange things people learn to go through to scrape up the daily bread. I can't picture a little kid with a burning desire to be a telephone interviewer when he grows up. Not me, I think. I'm one of the lucky ones. I'm a musician. Please God.

The first week goes by and now it's August. I start to get a leaden feeling. If Ryan was enthusiastic, he would have called right away, wouldn't he? But I could swear he liked us. He looked interested. That A&R man looked interested. I could swear . . . Maybe he's busy. Maybe a lot of other things came up.

I've sent the just-in-case deposit to Stony Brook. I dropped it in the mailbox with a feeling of unreality. Full tuition will be due soon. I haven't called any rehearsals. Out of Control is in limbo. There are a couple of weeks to go on my job at the school and I watch Jessica in the mornings, running in circles around the track. I'm immobile, waiting.

We sit in the bleachers, me with my before-work coffee and Jessica, sweating, drinking her little can of orange juice. She's broken up with Johnny.

"I'm sorry," she says. "I hope it doesn't disrupt the band."

"What's the story?" I say. "Are you on friendly terms or what?"

"I feel friendly," she says. "Oh God, 'friendly'! That's . . . we were very close. I want to keep his friendship. Johnny goes on and off, though."

"What do you mean?" Am I going to have to find another guitarist in a hurry? Just when Jessica was improving?

"Maybe you were right," she says, "about not getting involved with someone in the band. But it happened and— Well, we talk on the phone a lot. Sometimes it's okay and sometimes he yells at me. He gets kind of abusive and— He's hurt, I guess and—I don't know how he'd be in rehearsal."

"Johnny takes a lot of patience, that's for sure."

"He calls me at all kinds of strange hours, when he gets smashed. I don't know what's going on with him. My dad's getting mad and—"

"Listen," I say, "if Out of Control takes off, Johnny won't mess it up. He wants it as much as anybody. He'll have to control his feelings, that's all."

She looks at me, eyebrows raised. "Johnny? Control his feelings?"

I half laugh and shrug. "If Ryan wants us, Johnny will

be civilized. And if Ryan isn't interested, it's all over anyway."

"Besides, I didn't do anything terrible," she says. "High school romances break up. It happens all the time. They're supposed to break up, aren't they? It happens all the time."

"Yeah, sure," I say. "Why not?"

The phone is on the kitchen wall above the table. It rings just before dinner. I have a mouthful of celery that I've filched from the salad that Mom is making on the kitchen counter and she slaps my hand away. Frankie and George are fighting in the living room and Mom is yelling at them as she lifts the receiver.

"Stop it, you two! Stop it right now! . . . Hello? . . . Yes, just a minute." There are more screams from the living room. "For you, Darren."

"Hello?" I say. I swallow to get the celery out of the way.

"Darren, hello. Dennis Ryan here."

"Oh, hi," I say. There's still a lot of celery left and my speech sounds muddy. That's my heart starting to pump. "How are you?"

"Great. Just great." There's a little pause. "I meant to get back to you sooner, but—"

"Yeah, sure. That's okay." Please, God. Please.

"I want to tell you right up front, that's a good group you've put together. A lot of talent there. The guitar's a little weak, but she's a looker, all right."

"Jessica," I say. I think quick. I can replace her. I could get Gary Vernon. . . .

"It's a good group, but the truth is, your overall sound is not that *different.*"

"Oh." Mom's knife is making rhythmic chops against the wooden board. George is screaming at the top of his lungs in the living room.

"See, it's the *different* sound I'm looking for. So the group as a *whole* is not what I'm looking for, but—"

He wants me, just me, me alone. I'll talk to the guys, they'll understand and I—

"—but you and that singer are truly outstanding. You're a dynamite talent, Darren, no doubt about it. The bitch of it is I don't have a spot for keyboards right now. I'll definitely keep you in mind. I could fit the singer in with Double Exposure. That's the group I was telling you about, the one that's getting so much press, remember? Well, they're revamping a little and the singer could fit in very nicely."

"The singer," I say. "Johnny." My voice comes out a croak and Mom looks at me questioningly. I turn away and face the wall.

"Right, Johnny. He's got a quality. You know, that urgency—he sounds like Rod Stewart."

"But you wanted something different." Son of a bitch! The stupid son of a bitch! Damn stupid son of a bitch!

"Well, sure, different but not *too* different."

The paint on the kitchen wall is peeling. The sounds of Frankie and George wrestling in the living room are echoing in my ears. Salvage something, I think. Got to salvage something.

"The songs," I say, in that terrible croak. "What about the songs?"

"Well, that's what I mean. They're a shade *too* different. 'Botulism in Mom's Apple Pie'—now what is that, Darren? You're talented as hell, but the bottom line is the songs aren't commercial. Too complicated."

"Complicated? 'Now' isn't complicated. It's—" Dammit, stop begging.

"Right, that one. That might be commercial. I'm not kidding you, Darren. I'll definitely keep you in mind in case I hear of something. . . ."

"Thanks," I say.

"And I want to be up-front with you all the way. I don't know how you feel about losing Johnny. If you want to give him this opportunity, though, it's a big opportunity for him to—"

"That's okay," I say. "The band is breaking up anyway, college and—"

"So if you want to give me Johnny's number—"

"It's upstairs," I say. "I have to go get it." I take a deep breath. My damn voice is breaking!

"No need to go to any trouble. Is he in the book?"

"No, it's unlisted. Hold on a minute and I'll—"

"Tell you what. If he's interested, tell him to buzz me, okay?"

"Okay, sure."

"And I want to tell you right now, it was a real pleasure to hear your group."

"Yeah, sure."

I hang up and I stand there, facing the wall.

I hear Mom's voice behind me. "What was that? What's going on?"

"Nothing! Nothing!" I shout at her and watch her eyes widen. "Frankie's beating on George in there and you're listening to my phone calls! Why the hell don't you do something about Frankie instead?" I run down the hall into the bathroom and lock the door. I think I'm going to throw up. Johnny can't even read music! Johnny can't read a damn note of music!

The funny thing is I had a definite vision of the way it would be. I saw us looking over Ryan's contract, Johnny getting hyper and Mike checking out the fine print. I saw myself packing to go on the road, going out the front door, nervous and excited, hugging Mom good-bye. It was so real.

He wants something different, just like Rod Stewart! That's so funny, I could almost laugh. I wash my face with cold water. I splash a lot of cold water over my head. I can't come up with any lyrics to fit this one. I'll have to tell the guys. I'll have to tell Johnny. It can wait a day. Just a day.

I go through the motions: get up, go to work, eat. I'm not practicing anymore. For the first time since I was eight years old, I'm not practicing. It leaves a strange hole in the day. I walk around feeling like there's something I'm supposed to do and then I remember there's nothing. I sleep a lot. Sometimes I go to sleep right after dinner.

Every day is the day I'm going to call Johnny. A couple of times, I've gotten as far as turning to his number in my address book. Then I think, later, I'm tired from scrubbing those walls all day. Or, I want to work out a way to tell him, some way that doesn't make me sound like a pathetic ass. I have to tell the guys, too. Tom calls me all the time. I've started drinking my coffee at the deli to avoid the morning talks with Jessica.

I guess I'm embarrassed. I can't face anyone's pity or anyone's satisfaction at seeing the triple threat talent shot down. In a little while, I'll leave for orientation at Stony Brook. Tom will be off to Bard. It'll be easier to tell them just before I go; then I won't be stuck hanging around town with egg on my face. But I can't hold out on Johnny.

One night, I got to a party at Bill's. It's one of those big open-house things, four dollars at the door for the keg, with friends of friends of friends. The place is jammed. Mike is around someplace, Jessica is at the other side of the room with a bunch of people, I'm standing with Tom near the door. It looks like the whole town is here. I see Johnny come in. This is it, I think, I'm going to tell him right now.

"Hey, Johnny! Over here!" I wave at him. I can hardly hear myself over the blast from the stereo.

Johnny is working his way through the crowd toward me and Tom. I see him glancing around the room as he goes. Suddenly, he stops dead. His face freezes. I mean it, it gets blank like a mask and dead white. He turns right around and walks out fast.

"Johnny, wait!" I call after him. "I've got something to—" He never stops and then he's gone. Shit, I was going to get it over with. I was going to tell him and Tom right now.

"What the hell's wrong with him?" I say to Tom. "What did he take off like that for?"

"He saw Jessica," Tom says.

"What?"

"He does that. If he comes into a party and Jessica's there, he leaves right away."

"Why? Jessica says they talk on the phone and—"

"He can't take seeing her in public. He can't see her with other people. You know what she told me? He wants her to call him every night to tell him where she'll be, so he won't go there. He expects her to check in with him before she goes out."

"Is he freaking or what?"

"You think so, Darren?"

I can't figure out why Tom looks so upset about this.

"Well, you know Johnny," I say.

"It's just Johnny, right?" Tom echoes. "It won't last long, right?"

"And so what if Jessica's here?" I say. "At a party this large?"

"He'll get over it," Tom says. He seems uptight. "Johnny'll be okay. Sure, nothing ever bothers him that much."

Nothing else will matter when he hears about Ryan. He'll be ecstatic about going with Double Exposure. I'm going to call him the next chance I get. Very soon.

Mike

There was this girl, Melanie, in my French class last term. Fantastic looks, with long red hair and milk white skin. I didn't really know her. You can be in the same class all year with kids that you never actually talk to. I'd kill time checking her out—if Melanie was my girlfriend, I'd think, I'd burn all her Polos. I hate that faux old-English-money look. She'd be hot in something funky.

Mrs. Kessler used to mix the conjugations of arcane verbs with lectures on French culture. She was a dedicated Francophile with a Brooklyn accent; God only knows what she sounded like in French. One day she was hyped up about the French national character—artistic, literate, wine-drinking gourmets. . . .

When we filed out of the classroom, I passed by Melanie and heard her mutter "*merde.*"

I stopped in my tracks. "That's good. Very good."

"What?"

"Listen, if you can actually curse in a language, you've got it down."

Melanie looked exasperated. "It's those ridiculous generalizations. We lived in France for a year; Mrs. Kessler should have met our concierge. . . . Everyone walking along *la rue* is not a connoisseur of the fine arts."

"Yeah, but their political system is cool," I said. "I like all those splinter parties."

So we walked down the hall talking about it and she seemed mildly interested, but school ended soon after that and I didn't get to see her again.

Well, yesterday morning, I'm at Genovese picking up some light bulbs and there's Melanie at the cash register. So I hung around and we tried talking between her ringing up sales. It was very disjointed.

Finally she laughed and said, "Look, I have to work. . . . There's a party at my house tonight. If you'd like to come?"

"Sure! Great!"

"It won't start until late, though. Not until after midnight. It's kind of a cast party for *Kismet.*"

I didn't know she was in summer theater. I didn't know

much about her, but she kept getting more interesting. I still hated the way she dressed, though.

"What do you do in it?"

A woman with a Pampers-loaded shopping cart interrupted. "Are the coupons good for the jumbo size?"

"Yes." Ding, ding. "That's ten twenty-seven."

"Wait—I have two pennies somewhere. . . ."

"What do you do in *Kismet*?"

"Dance. I have one good scene and— Three forty-seven, sir."

"I never knew you were a dancer."

Ding, ding. "Fifty-three and one makes five. Thank you . . . Mike, I'll tell you about it later."

Between customers she jotted down her address. "You can bring a friend if you want," she said.

So Johnny was coming with me. I wasn't friendly with any of the kids in that theater crowd, so if Melanie was occupied, I'd have someone to talk to. Maybe she meant I could bring a *girl*friend; for all I knew, she was seeing someone. But then, she wouldn't have invited me, right?

There's a whole lot of time to kill until midnight. I thought of catching the show, but the community theater does warmed-over Broadway and it doesn't grab me. And the truth is, I'd rather take my Borodin straight. Anyway, Johnny wasn't into it. The show is on tonight, Friday night, Saturday night, and Sunday; if Melanie and I connect, maybe I'll go see it on the weekend.

I was meeting Johnny at the Three Deuces at nine. He got there ahead of me. I saw the blue Corvette in the parking lot and eased the bug right in next to it. I never hung out with him that much at night, just the two of us; I'm not that big a drinker. But I thought Johnny had slowed down a lot and, anyway, he's never boring.

I find him standing at the bar. The place is quiet. Thursday night, no band, so it's fairly empty.

We're talking for a while and looking around. He's restless. He tosses down two margaritas in a row, fast, like in the old days. It doesn't show on him. He can hold his liquor better than any guy I know.

"Let's get out of here," he says. "This place sucks."

We get into the cars and I follow him three blocks down the Boulevard to Bruno's. There's some kids from North Bay High in the back playing video games and some old guys at the bar. It's pretty quiet, too. We stand at the end of the bar. The bartender gives Johnny a big greeting. He checks my proof and it passes. I order a beer, Johnny throws down another margarita.

"Come on, let's cut out," he says.

"Wait," I say. I haven't even finished my beer. "Relax." He's very jumpy. He's not what you'd call deep, but he can be very funny. Not tonight, though.

I'm looking around to see if there's anyone else to talk to and then I see this girl coming through the door. She's got her hair in two little pigtails with yellow ribbons. She's wearing a well-endowed yellow-and-brown tiger-striped T-shirt.

"Look at that," I say.

She's with a girlfriend, but I only have eyes for the T-shirt. There's a deep V and she's actually spilling out of it.

"Man, she's built!"

He glances over. "I know her," he says. "She goes to St. Joseph's. She gave me a hand job once."

"What?"

They're passing our end of the bar, heading for the tables in the back, and she stops in front of us.

"Hi, Johnny."

"Hi," he says. "How're you doing? What's your name again?"

"Evie."

"Oh, right, Evie. Evie, my friend Mike here was just saying, it's the best pair he's ever seen."

I can't help it, I start blushing. I can't believe Johnny! I expect her to turn her nose up and walk away.

She looks at me and says primly, "Thank you."

You're welcome seems kind of inappropriate.

"You're the drummer, right?"

"That's me."

"This is my friend Janet. We saw your band at the Three Deuces, what was it, a couple of weeks ago?" she says. "We were right in front."

"Yeah," Johnny says. "We saw you. We noticed you right away, right Mike? Weren't you wearing a dress—what color was it again?"

"We had jeans," the other girl says, "and I had a white shirt."

"Right." Johnny nods. "I remember you. In the white shirt. Can we buy you girls a drink?"

"Sure," Evie says.

"No, wait, this place is beat," Johnny says. "Why don't we go to the house? I got some Glenfiddich."

"Oh. I don't know." They start consulting with each other.

Johnny is impatient. "Come on, let's go, this place serves swill."

Johnny's moving too fast and I'm sure he's going to lose them. It's just as well because—is he forgetting we're going to Melanie's?

"Well, okay," Evie says. "Let's go."

They walk out of Bruno's in front of us. Evie's denim skirt is packed solid.

"What are you doing?" I whisper frantically to Johnny. "We're going to *Melanie's*."

"Plenty of time. We'll hang out at the house for a while."

I check my watch. It's 10:30. Okay, we can hang out for an hour or so.

At the parking lot, we go through a whole number about they're leaving their car at Bruno's and we'll definitely drive them back.

"Listen, at the stroke of midnight," I tell Johnny. "No matter what."

"Anything wrong with me bringing a date to the party?" Johnny asks.

I shrug. "I don't know. I guess not."

"Which one do you want?" Johnny says. "Take your pick. You want Evie?"

"Hey, I don't want anyone!" I am not bringing some girl to Melanie's! "Listen, can we pass on this?"

"What's the other one's name again?"

"Janet." Janet is mousy—both in the sense of colorless and something rodentlike about her mouth.

"Hey Janet!" he calls. "I love you and don't you forget it!"

He's crazy tonight.

Johnny takes Janet into the Corvette. I'm left with Evie and Johnny gives me a wink.

Now I've got Evie next to me in the front seat and I'm driving along, following the Corvette. She's sitting close. Her perfume is sweet and heavy. She's sitting very close.

"You're good on the drums," she says.

"Thanks."

"You remind me of that drumer in Duran Duran." She smiles at me and there's a little gap between her front teeth. "I mean in looks."

Wait a minute! What am I going to do with her if Johnny takes Janet to the party? Just drop her off by herself at Bruno's? Listen, I'm a nice guy—so what do I do? I feel stuck. I have to get out of this.

"You're shy, aren't you?" she says.

"Not especially."

"I think that's cute."

We get to the house and we go out near the pool. We sit down on the padded white iron furniture Johnny's got there. Johnny turns on the waterfall and the girls go, "Oooooh." He goes in the house and brings out a bottle of scotch and we're passing it around. I skip my turn. Evie takes a good-sized swig. Johnny's got Janet on his lap on one of the chairs and I'm sitting next to Evie on this love seat. Johnny's kissing Janet and she's all over him. Evie looks at me expectantly. This is embarrassing.

Then Johnny stands up. He picks the bottle up off the table and offers it around. "Last chance," he says to me and Evie, "Janet and me are going in the house."

"I'll pass," I say. Evie takes another good gulp.

Johnny's carrying the bottle in one hand and he's got the other gripping Janet. I watch them go out of sight, into the shadows.

"Hey, you want to—uh—we could go inside?" Evie says.

"No." Pause. "It's nice and cool out here."

"I bet his house is air-conditioned. I bet there's lots of different rooms in there. We could like go inside."

She's coming on strong and I feel like a total idiot.

"Yeah, he's got air-conditioning," I say. I check my watch. Almost eleven. I could happily strangle Johnny.

Long, long silence. I have nothing to say to this girl.

"Are you just shy or gay? Because if you're just shy, like—uh—you don't have to be." She says this in a very understanding, maternal tone. In a peculiar kind of way, she's sweet.

Time drags by. Do I opt for being gay? No, this is crazy.

"Listen, Evie. I really like you and all that, but I've got plans for—there's someplace I have to be at midnight. By myself. So I'd love to—you know, go inside with you, but I'm going to have to drop you off in a little while. So it doesn't seem right," I finish lamely. In half an hour, I'm outa here—with or without Johnny.

She digests that silently. I can almost hear her thinking. Then, "You're being a gentleman, aren't you?"

"Well, I try."

"I understand. That's nice." She shifts her weight away from me in the love seat and faces me, looking serious. "You're nice and I want to tell you—I don't want you thinking I'd screw just anybody."

"Hell, no," I say. "I don't think anything."

"Because I don't," she says. "I don't screw everybody."

"Sure," I say. "I know that."

"Me and Janet, we only do rock musicians."

"What?"

"That's all. Just rock musicians. I've never done anybody else," she says. She sounds proud of her perfect record.

"That's great," I say. "That's like exclusive."

"The biggest," she says. "was Brian of the Alley Cats."

"The biggest?"

"The biggest star. I met him backstage at the Nassau Coliseum. I tried for Mick one time, but—"

"That's a nice hobby," I say, "almost like collecting autographs."

She beams at me. "Yeah, it's like that, only more personal." She looks around. "This is a nice place. You all live together here?"

"No. It's Johnny's house."

"Some of the groups live all together," she says. "I was with the Crimson Force one time and they all live together in a big mansion."

"Oh," I say.

"Are you guys recording?"

"No. Not yet."

"That's okay. I wouldn't have minded, honest," she says. "Don't feel bad about it. I mean, I like to do people at the very beginning of their careers. It's kind of like helping them get started."

"That's a generous attitude," I say. "You're a considerate person." It's true, if you look at it from her bizarre frame of reference.

"Thank you . . . I always like the drummers best," she says. "Because they're so well-coordinated."

I smile. "That alone makes all those music lessons worthwhile."

"Maybe we'll run into each other some other time," she says. "Anyway, it's nice talking like this."

We've fallen into a relaxed, companionable silence.

After a while, she sighs. "That's a beautiful pool."

"You should see it in the daytime. There's a Jacuzzi on the other side."

She stretches. "It *is* nice out here."

"Mmm-hmm," I say. The air is still and it smells green.

"I never learned to swim," she says. "I'm afraid to put my head underwater, you know?"

"That's too bad. You ought to try to get over that."

"I guess."

If Johnny doesn't show soon— Good thing I took my own car!

It's a cloudless night and the stars are out in force. I think I see a firefly. I can't remember the last time I saw a firefly.

"My cousin is on a swim team and . . ." The monotonous drone of her voice is soothing. ". . . and then she said . . ."

Too many times I've wanted to do something and everything conspires to derail me. I'm not getting derailed tonight. I'm definitely getting to Melanie's.

". . . so if I did the backstroke, my face would stay up out of the water . . ."

My eyes are closed and I'm half listening.

". . . but I told her . . . all summer and . . ."

I'm suddenly jarred by a scream.

"Evie! Evie!" It's Janet. She's running down the hill from the house.

"Evie! He's crazy!" She sounds hysterical.

"What?"

"Your friend!" Janet yells. "He's got a gun!"

I'm unfocused. "I know, so what?" I know where the rack is, right over the water bed. So what?

"Hey," Evie sits up straight. "What's going on?"

Janet is talking a mile a minute. Her eyes are wide. "He's nuts, that's what! First he finishes that bottle by himself, one, two, three, and he's calling it mother's milk. I mean, a quart! Then he gets some ludes. I only take a half; I don't see what he takes. He seems okay, maybe a little drunk, and we're like fooling around a little, and then the next thing I know, he's sitting there crying! The guy's crying, with real tears and noise! And then he takes his gun down and loads it! He's saying all this crazy stuff! Well, I ran out of there!"

"Is he in the house?" I say. What the hell is Johnny doing?

"I don't know," she says. "I don't know where he is. I just got out of there fast!"

"What's wrong with him?" Evie has jumped up.

"Nothing. Johnny's okay," I say.

Then I see him silhouetted up on the lawn. He's staggering and he's carrying something. Right, it's the rifle.

"Let's get out of here!" Janet says. "I want to get out of here!"

"Look at him," Evie says to me. "Let's go around the other way to the car."

"Wait a minute," I say. "I'll go talk to him."

"He might shoot you," Janet says. "What if he shoots you? Who's gonna drive us back?"

"Johnny's okay," I say. "Just wait a minute."

I leave them at the pool. I start up the lawn toward him. This is *Johnny*. I can't be scared of Johnny.

"Hey, Johnny?" I say softly.

"Leave me alone. Leave. Alone."

"It's Mike." I'm slowly moving closer to him. "What happened? It's Mike."

When I get close, I see tears streaming down his face. His face is contorted. He's making small, sighing noises deep in his throat.

"Take it easy. Hey, Johnny?"

He's staggering and waving the gun around.

"Johnny, give it to me, okay? What are you doing?"

"I'm gonna shoot down the damn moon!"

"What?"

"Jessica . . . What's moonlight to Jessica?"

"Hey, Johnny—"

He's talking and sobbing at the same time, hard to understand. I'm listening closely and missing every other word. ". . . Jessica . . . no feelings . . . you tell her . . . I'm gonna waste the moon!"

He's looking through the sight and he has the gun pointed straight up at the sky. He's weaving and his hand is on the trigger and the gun is swaying back and forth.

"Johnny, what's the range of that thing? Hey, don't! You could hit somebody across the bay! Johnny, don't!"

He fires and one of the girls screams. The recoil jerks him backward. Then he slumps down on the grass.

I half expect the moon to be shattered. I'm hoping he won't notice it's still up there. Some trip Johnny's on!

"Hey, take it easy," I say. I squat next to him. I take the gun from him and put the safety on. There's no resistance. His arms are limp.

My legs give way with relief. I stand there a minute

and take a deep breath. The smell of the lawn mixes with the metallic smell of powder.

Then I half lead, half carry him toward the house. I'm trying to say soothing things to him all the way. The tears are still streaming down. We get to the terrace steps and I can't get him to walk up. He sinks down on the first step, head in his hands.

"Come on in," I say. "Come on. You'll sleep it off."

He won't budge. He's a dead weight.

I go through the glass sliding doors and take the gun to his room. I unload it and put the bullets in my pocket. I rest it gently on the rack. I've never seen any guy crying like that. Johnny's always so cool. I've never seen anything like this. Jessica ought to see him now!

When I get back outside, he's sitting where I left him.

It's way past midnight!

"Come into the house," I say.

He mumbles something.

"Come on. You'll feel better. Go to bed."

I sure as hell can't carry him. Maybe I should let him sleep it off here.

"Johnny, are you okay?" I say. "You want to stay out here?"

Nothing.

"Listen," I say. "The girls want me to drive them back. I'd better get them back."

"Wasted the moon," he mumbles.

"Sure you did," I say. "Are you going to be okay?"

He looks straight at me. His face is all wet. "Go away," he says clearly.

He looks like he's going to be all right. He can sleep

it off out here. Actually, what's the difference? It's a warm night.

I have to get to Melanie's before the party breaks up!

"Come on," I call to the girls. "I'll drive you back."

They make a big cautious semicircle to avoid passing in front of Johnny. I get them into the car and before I drive off, I check him again. He's slumped over, motionless. He'll be okay here. I pull out onto the road. He'll think it's funny in the morning. He'll crack up when I tell him about it.

I speed down Shore Road.

"I thought he was going to kill me," Janet is whispering to Evie. "I was scared stiff. He was calling me names and—"

At Bruno's, Janet scrambles out of my car as fast as she can. She's afraid of me, too. I say good-bye to Evie and I pull out with a screech of the tires. I drive double time to Melanie's on the opposite end of town. I'm beating all the lights and keeping an ear out for sirens.

The hassle to get here was worthwhile. The party is lame, definitely in the slow lane, but Melanie is terrific. We spend most of the time sitting out on the patio, eating potato chips and laying out our lives to date, overlapping each other's stories. She's smart; she picks up immediately on everything I say. She's very funny. She's extremely pretty.

At one point, she tips her head up and looks at the sky. "It's such a clear night; just look at the moon!"

"Whew, it's still there!" I say. I start laughing.

"What?"

I'm on the verge of telling her about this weird evening

with Johnny, but I decide not to; it's one of those things where you had to be there.

I'm the last person to leave the party. I'm definitely going to see *Kismet* tomorrow night. Saturday and Sunday, too.

Jessica

I hear the garbage cans falling over in my sleep. I hear the clang of metal under my window. Raccoons again, I think. I'm too sleepy to do anything about it, though. I think the fluorescent hands on my bedside clock read ten past four, but I'm not sure. I'm too tired to really look or care. Clang. Raccoons. Someone will have to pick up orange peelings and wet paper wrapping in the morning. And I fall asleep again.

The next sound is something hitting the window next to my bed. "Damn raccoons!" and I fall back into a dream where I was pulling at a yellow velvet shawl as if it really mattered and there were staccato taps against glass. . . . And then I'm fully awake. It's not raccoons throwing pebbles at my windowpane.

I push the blinds out of the way. It is that moment just before it gets light and gray night shadows are still hanging on to everything in the yard. The redwood table is a dark mass looming in the half-light. His white shirt stands out against the gloom and I see Johnny. His posture looks peculiar. I open the window wide and lean out.

"Johnny?"

"Help me." His voice sounds very hoarse. "Help me, Jess."

"Wait. I'll be right down."

I feel thick with sleep and my heart is pounding. I've been sleeping in a T-shirt. I pull on the first thing I see, a pair of running shorts hanging on the back of my swivel chair. I rush down the stairs, softly, barefoot. I open the back door, not letting it creak. The clock over the kitchen counter says 4:25. I push the button on the door so that it stays unlocked and I close it quietly.

Johnny is stumbling around in the yard. "Jessica!"

I reach him and I smell the liquor. His shirt is torn at the shoulder. At first I think it's bloody and then I realize that it's smears of dirt.

"Jessica!"

"Ssshh," I say. "Don't wake everybody."

"I want to talk to you!" His voice is loud, with that hoarse, torn sound again.

He's going to wake Mom and Dad and the whole neighborhood.

"I have to talk to you, damn you!"

The torn, dirty shirt and the pained look on his face shut off my anger.

"Ssshh," I say. "We'll go sit in the car, okay?"

How did he get here? My God, he can't even walk!

"The car's up the hill." His speech is slurred.

By "up the hill," I think he means around the corner on Hillview Road. I try to support him and guide him down the driveway. He can hardly stand up and I almost lose my balance. His face is gray.

"Don't push me!"

"Ssshh. Come on, Johnny."

"Don't friggin' push me!" He shakes me off roughly.

"Johnny, what should I do? What do you want me to do?"

"I want to talk to you!"

"Okay, in the car. Come on."

I steer him toward the road. Pebbles dig into my feet.

"Help me, Jess."

The car is parked just a little way up the hill, in front of the Gordons' house. It's parked near the curb and it looks all right. It doesn't look like an accident. I'm relieved when we get inside and I close the door. I wish I was old enough for a license. I wish I could drive and get him home. Maybe he could sleep it off in the car. The car, Johnny, everything reeks of liquor.

"Johnny, give me the keys."

"No."

"Please, Johnny. Give them to me."

I wish I had brushed my teeth. My mouth tastes terrible.

"I'll hold them for you," I say.

"No. No way." He looks at me suspiciously and for the first time, I see how strange his eyes look. His face is colorless, all the blood drained out.

"How did you drive over here?" I say. "You could have killed yourself."

"I could have killed myself," he repeats. "Know what I could do?"

"What?"

"See that post?"

There is a stone post on the lawn directly down the hill from us. It holds a lantern that is dark now. All the lights are out along the street and everything is still.

"Could step on the gas and drive into that post. That's what I could do. Take care of all our problems."

I don't know where the keys are. Maybe in his pocket. At least they're not in the ignition.

"I could kill both of us right now," he says.

"Johnny, please . . ."

"Your fault," he says. "Drinking to forget you."

Drinking to forget you. That sounds so phony. It would make me laugh if I heard it somewhere else, if I wasn't getting so scared.

"You messed with my mind. If I die, it's all your fault."

"Johnny, please, don't get weird. . . ."

"I love you! Dammit, I friggin' love you!" His voice is raspy. "I'm gonna wind up in some loony bin because of you!"

"Johnny, what did you do? How much did you drink?"

"I don't know. Don't know what I took."

"What?" I feel chilled. "Johnny, did you take anything?"

He's mumbling.

I'm remembering something he told me. Long ago, he'd said, before he was so happy with me, he'd said. He'd experimented, mixing drinking with meth. Or was it mesc? Methedrine or mescaline? I don't remember which. Or Laurel's ludes or what else?

He's ghostly pale.

"What did you take?" I'm almost yelling at him.

"Don't know. I don't know."

"Johnny, I'll get somebody!" I should get him to an emergency room. North Shore Emergency. I don't know. What do I know? "I'll get my dad, I'll—"

"No! No!" He's yelling at me.

"Johnny, let me call somebody."

"No!"

"Tell me what to do. I don't know what to do."

"Don't leave me, Jess. Stay with me."

I'm probably imagining things. What if I called Mom and Dad, or Johnny's father, and it turned out that he was only drunk? But what if . . . I'm starting to cry. I put my hand up to my face to wipe my eyes.

"What're you doing? Who're you waving at?"

"I'm not."

"Who're you signaling?"

"Nobody. I'm just—"

"Dammit, you're waving at somebody! Who's back there?"

"No one. There's no one." I'm making an effort to keep my voice calm. "It's all right, Johnny."

"Cut it out! Cut it out or I'm gonna ram this car into that house across the street with both of us in it and—"

Is he hallucinating? I don't know what to do. I don't want anyone to see him like this.

He has slumped down, his head in my lap.

He's mumbling and I make out scattered words. ". . . what you've put me through . . . bitch . . . love me . . ."

I watch him breathing. He's breathing. I hope he's sleeping. I'm thinking a million things. Unconscious. A coma. Brain dead. It would be just like Johnny to come here to make me watch him die. Oh God! I'm crying soundlessly.

He starts. "Where're you going? Don't leave me, Jess."

"I'm here," I say.

His head feels heavy on my lap. I can't move. My legs are stiff. The night has not relieved yesterday's mugginess. My T-shirt is collecting the humidity.

"I can't deal with it," he says. "I could kill you for . . ." And he's out again.

I watch the sky getting lighter.

I watch him breathing. I watch the color of his face. He looks so terrible. Maybe it's alcohol poisoning. How can you tell if it's alcohol poisoning? I don't know what I'm supposed to look for. I'm paralyzed and standing guard over him. I cry soundlessly and watch for the color in his face.

I shift my knees under him and roll down the window. The smell of grass cuts through the hot, stale air of the car. Green smells, green sounds. The peaceful rustling of leaves. Something buzzing nearby.

His breathing sounds better. I think he's sleeping. I think he's all right. Oh please, let him be all right.

If something happened to Johnny . . . All those car crashes happened before he ever knew me. It's not me. It's not my fault. It's Johnny. It's not my fault. I'm sixteen years old. I'm allowed to break up with someone. It's not my fault.

His color looks closer to normal. I wipe my eyes. I think I've been crying for hours.

I'm sure he's sleeping now, his mouth relaxed and open a little. His face, asleep is so very familiar. I guess I love him, in a way. I could never go out with him again, though. I'd be afraid to ever break up with him again.

I feel heavy with exhaustion. My eyes hurt. I need to sleep, too.

It's almost light. Mr. Gordon is coming out of his house,

wearing a business suit. He must be going to work already. He passes by the car and he doesn't see me. Or maybe he's being nice and pretending not to see me. Pretty soon, everyone in the neighborhood will be up and going to work. Dad, too. I'm not even wearing any underwear!

I slowly ease out from under. He doesn't wake up. I rest Johnny's head on the seat cushion. He's breathing evenly and I'm sure he's sleeping. He'll be okay here. I'll go home and sleep for a while and then I'll get dressed and check on him later. I hate to think of him waking up here, alone, in a torn, dirty shirt. Johnny cares so much about being immaculate.

Johnny

The phone is ringing and I want to crawl away someplace. I sure hope I had a great time to match this head I've got.

The damn phone is still ringing off the hook, so I finally pick it up.

"Hello."

"Johnny? It's Jessica."

Right away I feel that gladness I always get from hearing her voice. *It's Jessica.* I friggin' know it's Jessica, nobody sounds just like her. I'm waking up happy. And then I remember we're not together anymore and it hits me, hard, like a bulldozer, all over again. I take a breath. But she's calling me, so maybe, maybe . . .

"Jess?" I say.

"Listen, I'm glad you made it home all right. I woke up a little later and the car was gone, so . . ."

"Yeah, sure," I say. I don't know what she's talking about.

"Well, okay. So long."

I need to keep her on longer.

"Wait a minute," I say. "What time is it anyway?"

"One."

"One, like in the afternoon?"

"Sorry if I woke you. I had to know if—"

"Hey, Jess?" I reach for a cigarette and light it. It makes me want to puke and I grind it out. "Jess, remember that time I called your house at six? That first week we started going out. That was so funny."

"I remember," she says.

"I'd been out with the guys and I called you when I woke up. I thought it was six at night, so I called you, remember?"

"Yes," she says. She sounds like she's going to hang up.

"So your dad answers the phone and goes, 'Six on a Sunday morning! Can't it wait?' Man, I felt like some kind of freak. That was so funny. He was mad and I was apologizing all over the place, trying to make a good impression and—"

"I know. I was there," she goes. She's not laughing. "Listen, Johnny, I've got to go. I just wanted to be sure you were okay."

"Sure I'm okay, except for wanting you back. How do you mean, am I okay?"

There's a long silence on the other end. Finally she goes, "You don't remember last night, do you?"

I light another cigarette and manage to take a drag of

this one. I'm too hot. I forgot to turn the air-conditioning on, but even in this heat, I'm getting a cold, clammy ball in my stomach.

"Yeah, I remember last night," I say. "I was at Bruno's with Mike. Why? Did you come in later, did I say something or what?"

Another silence, and then her voice comes shooting at me through the receiver. "You were at my house at four in the morning. You don't remember any of it?"

"Hey, no. What happened? Jess, did your folks—"

"No. I was the only one you woke."

"Oh, wow. Well, that's okay then. . . . Hey Jess, I'm sorry."

"Do you remember driving home?"

"No." Not knowing—that's scary. It's like someone else has taken over for me.

"You're lucky, that's all I can say. If you don't care about killing yourself, you could have killed somebody else. For all you know, you might have run over somebody."

"It don't affect my driving." Everybody gets drunk sometimes. It's not such a big thing.

"Don't you ever come to me when you're stoned like that! I'm not going to baby-sit you! Not ever again!" Her voice is cutting me up.

"Jess, I'm sorry. Hey, Jess? I'm sorry. . . . I don't remember."

"Good-bye, Johnny," she goes.

"Wait, Jess! Don't be mad at me. What happened?"

"I thought you were dying." I hear her catching her breath. "I really thought so. You had me crying all night."

"I'm sorry, Jess. You know I'd rather cut off my right

arm than make you cry. You know that, don't you?" I mean it, too. I ought to cut something off to show her, like that crazy painter cut off his ear.

Silence at the other end.

"Jessica, I feel like shit. I was drunk. I'm sorry."

She was crying on account of me. I know she really loves me, in her heart. I'm gonna get her back just like it used to be. It's impossible for me to love her so much and not have her feel the same. It's not natural.

"Hey, Jess? When we get back together, I won't drink like that. It's only because I miss you so much and—"

"Stop it! Stop making me feel guilty! If you've got problems—"

"I don't have no problems. You're my problem."

"Don't, Johnny."

"You don't understand the way I love you. How am I supposed to be without you?"

Silence.

"Someday you're gonna look back and have big regrets, because this is once in a lifetime. Jess, no one's ever gonna love you the way I do. You're not mature enough to—" I'm fighting for my life.

"I don't want to hear this again," she says.

"Is there somebody else? Is it because of the snake?" She knows I mean Darren.

"No. I've told you and told you. No."

"Then I don't understand why. I love you, Jessica."

There's a long, long silence. I'm imagining the vanilla smell of her. I can see her sitting on the bed, holding the phone, wearing nothing but sheer bikini underpants, her silly pink ones that say Bloomie's. I'm almost sick with wanting her. I almost can't talk from wanting her.

Thinking about her makes that cold, clammy feeling go away.

Finally she says, "I can't talk anymore. Good-bye, Johnny." She almost sounds like she's crying again.

I'm going to send roses over to her today. And maybe candy, too. Something funny so she won't be mad anymore. A giant chocolate kiss, she'd like that. I can tell she cares. I can hear it in her voice. It's going to be just like it used to be. I can't understand why she's resisting it so much. Unless it's because of Darren coming on to her. It's because of Darren that all this stuff, this blackout shit, is happening to me. And Jessica, too. Jessica is doing this to me, too.

Jessica

There's an avalanche of things coming for me—flowers, candy, greeting cards, even a bouquet of helium balloons (of course, they say "I love you"). There's something almost every day. I don't know what to do with it.

I think Mom finds his persistence romantic. "Jessica, his love for you could be a once-in-a-lifetime—"

I physically jump as I interrupt her. "Are you writing Johnny's dialogue or is he writing yours?" And I'm afraid they might both be right.

She is less impressed with the phone calls in the middle of the night. And Dad is getting good and mad.

I'm training myself to grab for the receiver at the first ring, out of a dead sleep, before Dad is awakened.

"Hello."

"I told you to quit—" He starts off shouting at me.

"It's two o'clock in the morning!"

"I told you, quit hanging out with Mike and Tom and those guys!"

"What?"

"I called Mike to go out, and they were all going to that party with *you*. So what am I supposed to do? I get stuck doing nothing. Stay away from my friends!"

"Johnny, be rational."

"Don't give me this rational." (The last of the helium balloons is bobbing along my ceiling.)

"They're my friends, too," I say. "It was a big party. You could have gone."

"I can't see you in public! You know damn well I can't!" I hear the pain through his anger. I can't stand feeling so guilty all the time.

"Barbara and Darren still go to the same places. I can't see why—"

"Because I love you! It's different! I love you!"

"I can't see why we can't be civil."

I wonder what happens if Darren calls rehearsal. Well, luckily he hasn't. Maybe by the time he does, Johnny will get normal and we'll be able to be friends.

"What am I gonna talk to you about in front of people—the weather? Yeah, nice to see you here, Jessica. So how about this weather, Jessica?"

"I guess this town is too small for both of us." I'm trying to be funny, but it falls flat.

"Bitch!"

"Leave me alone, Johnny," I say. I am worn out.

"You leave my friends alone!" Furious click.

Another night. The phone interrupts my sleep in the

very early morning. I see pale gray light begin to seep around the edges of my curtains.

"Hello," I say wearily.

"Jessica, listen—"

"I'm going back to sleep," I say.

"No, wait—listen. Are you all right?"

"What? Yes, I'm all right. What—" My throat feels dry and scratchy.

"I dreamed about you. You were lying down and there were roses all around you, dark red roses, at your feet and around your head, and I thought you were . . ." His voice is torn and husky. I don't think I want to hear this, but I am mesmerized by his words. "You looked so beautiful. . . . You were white as a sheet. . . . I kept smelling the roses. . . . I touched your arm. . . . It was cold and limp. . . ."

"So you had a dream," I say coldly. A really creepy feeling is washing over me. "Good-night, Johnny."

"Wait! Jess! I love you! I love you so much! You're okay and that means we have another chance to—"

"No, don't." I think I hear him sobbing. I have feelings for him, I can't help it. . . .

"Jessica, I love you."

"I'm going back to sleep," I say. My hand is shaking as I put down the receiver.

Tom

I step on the bathroom scale and it reads 245! This is the first time I've been below 250 in years. I knew it! I knew I could do it, and this is only the beginning.

It's almost the end of summer and I'm glad. It's been a rotten summer and I'm going to leave it behind. Fall should be the new year instead of January. Fall seems like a fresh start and this year more than ever. At Bard, I have no history. I'll be a normal-looking guy who plays good bass. I'll probably join a band or something and meet a lot of people. Darren hasn't said anything, so I guess the thing with Ryan fell through. Well, I can live with that. I'm looking forward to college. And I'm getting it together. I know I can do it this time.

I feel hunger pangs this morning and I don't mind. I honestly don't. I'm going down to have breakfast in a minute and I'm having exactly what they said at the clinic: half a grapefruit, one slice of whole wheat toast, hard-boiled egg, coffee with skim milk, no sugar, a vitamin pill. And I'm going to get up from the table, still feeling hungry, but I can take it.

Later I'm going to Jones Beach with Jessica and everybody. I'll have to remember to pack a bag of fruit to help me keep away from the fast food. Maybe I'll even take off my T-shirt and get tan on my chest.

Everybody came—Jessica, Mike, Annie, Dale, Jimmy, Ray, that whole crowd, except for Johnny. This could be the last good beach Sunday for everyone to be together.

Darren's not here. Come to think of it, I haven't seen much of Darren lately. I wonder what he's been doing.

We're crowded on two blankets. Mike starts passing the beer around and it's hard not to be sociable. So I ask Jessica if she feels like taking a walk down the beach. When we get out of earshot, I tell her.

It helps to have Jessica to talk to again, someone I can trust like that.

"No more beer," I tell her. "At the clinic, they said no empty calories. You know what? I lost seven pounds so far. It probably doesn't show yet but—"

"That's great! You'll see, you'll look and feel so much better." The guys would probably laugh, but Jessica's always encouraging. It's good to be close to her again. When she was with Johnny, I felt like a third wheel.

"I'm even thinking of running with you some morning," I say.

"You're on. How about tomorrow?"

"Not yet. As soon as I drop some more pounds. You know what I mean, the track's too public."

"No one would care, Tom. But first, you have to get good running shoes. It's important—"

"Yeah, I will. They said to get a lot of exercise, to change my metabolism rate and . . ."

We've gone past the lifeguard station at Field 2. We're walking at the water's edge, our feet splashing through the surf. It becomes less crowded as we go.

"I'm proud of you, Tom. I really am."

"I've been walking a lot and yesterday I was swimming laps at Johnny's and—"

She stops and looks out at the ocean. "How does he seem to you?"

"Johnny? How do you mean?"

She's looking down at the ground, digging her toes into the damp sand.

"I'm . . . uncomfortable, Tom. I don't know what to do. Does he seem all right to you? He sent something strange to me."

"What?"

"Remember that time at Darren's—no, I forgot, you weren't there. One night at Darren's, we were listing things that were important to us—it was one of those games—and Johnny wrote One. Jessica. Two. Jessica. Three. Jessica. That was when we had first started going out and it was kind of cute. Well, yesterday, I got this fat envelope in the mail. There were four loose-leaf pages all folded up and he had written on both sides of each page, every line, in small print. It said One. Jessica. Two. Jessica. Three. Jessica. Four. Jessica. Tom, he got all the way up to eight hundred, eighty-two!"

She looks up at me. Next to us, a little girl is darting in and out of the water, screaming and running back each time a wave comes.

"Don't tell this to anyone, Tom. I don't want anyone talking about him. Promise."

"I won't say anything."

"That's all there was. Not another word. My name, eight hundred, eighty-two times."

"Come on, you know how Johnny is," I say hollowly.

Now the little girl is clutching her father's hand and she holds her ground as a wave pounds against her legs.

"He goes off the deep end once in a while," I say. "It doesn't mean anything. It'll blow over."

I'd gone over to Johnny's house the day before, to use

the pool. He knew I was coming, but he took a long, slow time to open the door. He was wearing the underwear he'd slept in and he needed a shave. He looked like hell. He sat at poolside, but he didn't swim. He said his stomach was hurting. He was sweating in the sun, squinting, chain-smoking and dropping the butts into a half-filled can of Coke. He looked seedy in the midst of all the Ocean Point splendor. He might be on downers again. I don't know. He used to take that stuff as casually as I take aspirin.

I never would have expected Johnny to suffer. I never meant any harm. The things I said just came out. We're like brothers; I mean, it's not like I planned to hurt him.

"He'll get over it," I say. "He'll be okay." He will, I tell myself. He can get a million girls. He doesn't need Jessica.

We start walking again, circling around someone with a fishing line. The lifeguard station is hazy in the distance.

Jessica's off in her own thoughts and I look at her beside me. She's wearing the pink bikini and her tan has become deep gold. The sun is behind her, making a halo around her hair. Her hair is growing in, too; she looks much softer. She's so beautiful! I want to reach out and take her hand. I'd like to walk along the beach holding hands with Jessica, not talking, swinging our hands and touching— I know I can't have that. But there'll be other girls, college girls who won't have the memory of me as the blimp. Maybe girls almost as pretty. I'll get into shape and start a new life.

"Let's jog back," she says.

I hesitate for a moment and then I think, the hell with it, so what if someone sees me!

"Okay," I say.

We do a slow jog. I'm not used to running barefoot in sand. My feet sink with each step. We're down near the water's edge, where it's bumpy and uneven. I concentrate on watching out for holes.

On the way home, crowded in the car between Jessica and Mike, I can feel the muscles in the back of my legs start to ache. It's a good ache. It makes me feel strong. And I'm down to 245! I'll run, I'll swim, I'll follow that clinic diet to the letter, and I'll make it! I feel in charge of myself.

I wake up and I feel as bad as the night before. I'm not sleeping right. I got to get rid of the water bed. The inside of my eyes hurts. I got to get myself together. I got to talk to Jessica and convince her. The way it is, she's wrecking my life.

I call Jessica. Even dialing the phone is a hassle. I get a wrong number and then I get her mother. Jessica's in the shower. She's never there when I want her! I tell her mother to have her call me right away. I tell her it's important.

I wait.

I have half a cup of coffee and it don't taste right. I think the milk's gone sour. I ought to get over to Dairy

Barn, but I don't feel like it. I'm wiped out. I got to get some energy flowing. Laurel's got that candy dish of ludes on her dresser—no more of that shit for me. I'm through with that. I've got to pep up.

Dust is supposed to fry your brains, but just this once won't hurt. Just this one time to get myself going. Just to get out of this rock-bottom low and then I won't do any more.

I try Jessica again. Her mother answers.

"Oh, I'm sorry, Johnny. She just left."

"Left? Where?"

"She went to the pool."

"But she was supposed to call me!"

That's just like her! She didn't even call back! She could have come over to my house if she was so friggin' hot to go swimming.

"What pool?"

"North Bay. Johnny, is something wrong?"

You're damn right something's wrong. Something's wrong with your daughter, lady. I can picture her, in that light pink bathing suit, fooling around in the water with Darren and laughing.

I can't sit around. The walls are caving in on me. Everything's caving in. I have to get out. I take the Corvette. That's supposed to make me feel good. Baby blue, shining, brand-new, still with that new car smell. I wish I'd waited for the black one, though. I never wanted a blue car. Black would be better. Or maybe red. "Little Red Corvette," like in the song. That would make me feel better. Nothing's any good anymore and it's her fault. She's putting me through this.

I drive over to the Boulevard and down to the Bay. I

drive around in a big circle—Shore Road, Main Street, East Drive. Some bastard cuts me off at the intersection. Back to Shore Road. I turn the radio on. I switch around until I get some up-tempo rock and I turn up the volume. It beats through my head like an anvil. Someone's blowing their horn at me. The sound goes into my head and turns into a ribbon of color. This car moves like a dream. It almost goes by itself. It goes straight to the parking lot for the public pool. There's something I'm supposed to do there.

Darren

The other day, Tom was telling me that he's worried about Johnny. I don't know, I can't see getting so concerned about Johnny moaning over Jessica. It sounds pretty stupid to me.

Anyway, I have just the thing that's going to make his day.

There's no point in stalling. It's ridiculous. I'm going to tell Johnny to call Dennis Ryan. No speeches, no story.

His phone is busy. Damn! I wanted to get it over with.

I wait a few minutes and dial again. It's ringing. No answer. I let it ring and ring. I must have just missed him.

Jessica

I haven't been to the North Bay pool all summer. I'd forgotten how noisy and crowded it gets. The little kids' voices and screams echo all around. I'm stretched out on a lounge next to Annie and there's a mother and her little girl right next to me on the other side. The kid is whining for something. The water is wall-to-wall people. Even the lanes are full. It's a big change from the waterfall in Ocean Point, that's for sure.

"I don't remember it being this bad," I say to Annie.

"You know what it is? All the camps are finished. That's why there are so many kids. Last week of summer is always the worst." She's leafing through the new copy of *Vogue*. "Look at this. Everything's going to be animal prints this fall. . . ."

I glance at the page. There's a steady stream of people crossing in front of us. An obese woman with crinkly thighs pouring out of a skirted print suit. Some tacky ruffled bathing caps. A man covered with curly black hair—arms, chest, and *back*. I decide the beautiful people don't hang out at public pools. That's what I'm thinking when I see him come in. He stands out because he's in clothes among all the half-nude bodies. Annie spots him, too.

"Isn't that Johnny? He must be looking for you."

He's looking around. What now, I think. I feel myself tensing. I should wave to him or something, I guess, but I don't. He spots me soon enough, anyway.

"Where's Darren?" he says.

"What?"

"You heard me. Where's Darren?"

"Don't say hello," Annie says. He ignores her.

"How am I supposed to know where Darren is?" I'm not in the mood for this.

"I want to talk to you!" He's too loud and angry, and the woman sitting next to me stares at us.

The pool attendant comes over with his no-street-clothes-at-the-pool spiel.

"Okay! All right!" Johnny starts to unbuckle his belt. He's pulling down his jeans and he's wearing nothing underneath. It would be funny, except I have a feeling he's not doing it to be smart-alecky. I have a feeling he's completely unaware. . . .

"What the hell do you think you're doing?" The pool attendant is one of those macho jocks from school. He's ready and eager to hassle someone. People all around are looking.

"Come on, Johnny," I say. "Pull your jeans up. I'll talk to you outside." I'm getting into my shorts and sneakers fast.

"A wise guy, huh?" The attendant is ready for a fight.

"Please. Give me a minute," I say "We're leaving."

"Should I wait here or what?" Annie says.

"No, dammit, don't wait for her! I'm driving her home!" Everything Johnny says sounds furious. He looks terrible.

Annie gives me a look. "It's okay," I tell her. "I wanted to go anyway."

At least Johnny has his jeans on again. I see a woman

from Mom's garden group watching the whole scene. I want to get Johnny out of here.

We go through the covered area that leads to the lockers and to the exit. It's dark in contrast to the bright sunlight. There's a piercing odor of chlorine.

"Why didn't you call me?" he says. "I was stuck waiting the whole damn day!"

"I'm sorry," I say. "Annie was picking me up and I was late and—" I'm more apologetic than I should be. His tone is making me nervous. There's a small dark tunnel leading to the women's lockers. For some reason, every horror movie I've ever seen comes back to me and I almost feel a shiver. Then I think, nothing can happen here. Not with all these kids' voices and mothers and babies splashing and— We pass by the tunnel and the sun is bright. Everything is so normal.

We're out in the parking lot now. We stand to the side, near the bike rack, out of the way of a car turning into a space.

"All right," I say. "What do you want to talk to me about?"

"What?"

"You pulled me out of the pool to say something. Okay. What is it?"

He stands looking at me, confused, and the silence lasts several beats too long. It chills me and I'm almost relieved when he starts ranting.

"You were supposed to call me back! You're always doing that to me!"

"Johnny, I just told you—"

"You got some kind of bug up your ass, you got to come to this pool? What's the matter with my pool?"

"Nothing, but—" I say.

"Yeah, because Darren's here, right? Darren's here!"

"He's not here."

"It's always Darren!"

"Where?" I say. "Where is he? Show me where he is."

"Then who is it? Who is it now?!"

There are people in the parking lot staring at us. I'm crazy to try to argue with him.

"Come on, keep it down," I say softly.

"Don't tell me what to do!"

"Okay, yell. Let's put on a show for everybody."

"I was so good to you. I was so *good* to you!" His face is contorted.

I hate seeing him like this. I hate feeling so guilty.

"Nobody's ever going to love you like I do! I *love* you!"

The words are the same. I've heard them before, around and around in circles. It's the hoarse way he's shouting that upsets me. I see some friends of my brother's on the steps to the pool. The shouts have made them look our way.

"Okay," I try to say calmly. "I know that. You've told me. I'm going home now." I start to walk away. I don't want to go back to the pool to ask Annie for a ride. I'll walk. It's not that far, not if I take the shortcut through the sand pits.

He grabs my arm. His fingers are digging into my flesh; I know there'll be a bruise tomorrow. "Come in the car. I want to talk to you."

"No thanks," I say. He's hurting me. I wish I had asked Annie to come out with me. I wish—

"Come on!"

"No!" I try to pull away and he yanks me hard. I lose my balance. I hear my shirtsleeve ripping.

"You think you're stronger than me?" he says. "You think you can pull away?" He's holding my shoulders tight and shaking me.

"Let me go!" How can I be scared? It's *Johnny*!

"You're wrecking my life! I want you to listen to me!" He looks as if he hates me. I've hurt him that much!

Larry's friends have come closer. "Are you okay, Jessica?" one of them calls.

I hesitate. Johnny relaxes his grip, but just slightly. He's scaring me. . . . But if my brother's friends interfere, Johnny will fight. He'll get into a fight and they'll pulverize him. He'll be on the ground, with his face bloodied and—

Long pause. Johnny is watching my face.

"No problem," I say. "Just a friendly argument." I can handle this. It's only Johnny.

"You're sure?"

I nod. "It's cool."

"Okay. Just checking." They move away. One of them looks back at me and then they disappear inside the pool entrance.

I wish Annie was here.

Johnny stares after them. "Who were those guys? There's always some guys! I could kill you for—"

His hold on my arms has loosened, and with a quick pull, I get away. I start to run. He looks in no condition to follow me. I go into a slow run and I cut across the parking lot. I'm upset. I want to be at home. There's a dirt path lined with beach grass that leads into the sand pits. If I stay on the path across the sand pits, I'll come out on Dogwood Road, three blocks from home.

I'll phone Tom or Mike or somebody. Somebody's got to take care of Johnny.

I reach the dirt path. I look over my shoulder. No sign of him, but I keep up a slow run anyway. I never go this way. It makes me uncomfortable. They say there are rats in the sand pits. And it's private property, posted with NO TRESPASSING signs.

The dirt ends and the path turns to sand. I run more slowly. The sand is coarse and tan. They say most of New York City was built with cement made from North Bay sand. Here's where the sand-mining operation is and the reclaimed section is where they built the pool. And then it goes up to the cliff where the mining hasn't started yet. You can see the Throg's Neck Bridge from the top of the cliff. The junior high kids come up here to drink beer. I wonder if Johnny did, in junior high. Something's gone so wrong with Johnny.

The cliff looms above me and I stay on the lower path that will take me to Dogwood. I'm breathing hard. My sneakers sink into the sand and I slow to a walk—and that's when I first notice the sound of the motor. Maybe it's one of the trucks, maybe they're working on this side of the pits—but I know it's not, even before I look.

I can't believe it. Johnny's driving the Corvette on the dirt path. He's coming after me! I start to run again and I hear nothing but my own harsh breathing, the crunching of sand underfoot, and the motor coming closer. He'll have to stop when he reaches the sand, I think—but he doesn't. Is he crazy? He's driving the Corvette into the sand! I run harder. My ribs start to ache. Then I hear the car stall behind me. A wheel must have sunk into the sand. I hear him cursing and gunning the engine. He's rocking the car. I'm running as fast as I can.

I hear a whine as the car starts up again. He's going to destroy it in the sand. He's going to destroy me. Suddenly, I know. He's going to run me down. I manage a new burst of speed and my lungs are burning. I am breathing sand particles. My shoes are sinking and my legs hurt. And all the time, I hear the car coming after me. It stalls again, more curses, and then I hear it straining to start. The car is groaning and it keeps on coming.

I've reached the fork where the low path meets the path that curves around the cliff. The low path means home but I can't outrun a car. The other path goes gradually uphill to the very top of the cliff. That has to stop him. No time to think. I take the uphill way. Again the car stalls behind me and I run on and on, winding higher and higher. I don't hear anything but my breathing for a long time, but I'm afraid to stop. And what if he gets out of the car— And what if—

All the training I've ever done was for this. All those mornings at the track are my chance to get away now. My legs scream with pain and I force them forward. And I hear the car start again.

I get to the top of the cliff. I never thought beyond this. I have nowhere to go from here. This is it. This is the top. This can't be happening. This is something I read about in newspapers. It can't be happening to me. I am panting and my legs are cramped. I can't run anymore. There is no place left to run. I hear the motor.

I give up. I sag against the old retaining wall and I see the car come into sight.

Split seconds become drawn out. Everything is uncommonly clear and illuminated. Fractions of seconds, and I see everything. The car has reached the flat section on top. It's me and the car. The car is picking up speed. Me and the car. Mommy, Daddy, Larry! I stare at the front grille, transfixed. Fractions of seconds. I remember an opossum caught in the glare of our headlights once. The opossum stood motionless, hypnotized in the path of the moving car. I am sobbing. I've wet my pants. My mouth tastes of grit. I wait, motionless. Time is splintering. I see Johnny through the windshield. Our eyes meet. Johnny's eyes lock into mine. The car is going full speed toward me. Johnny's eyes. Too late to stop. Too late. And suddenly, Johnny violently turns the steering wheel. He swerves past me and drives over the cliff. I see the car going over and over.

When I am finally able to move, I see it where it has hit the ground far below. It is crumpled and turned on its side, like a child's discarded toy.

It bursts into flames. The flames are bright blue and orange against the green of the shrubbery. My legs give way. I fall to my knees. I hear my voice screaming.

"Johnny!

"Johnny!

"Johnny!"

Jessica

Later, people said it was a very tasteful funeral. I don't know. I have no basis for comparison. It was my first one.

Johnny's father and Laurel brought the baby. He didn't squirm all that much for a two-year-old. He used to be just a blob to me. At the funeral, I realized he looks a lot like Johnny. A lot, especially around the mouth. I wonder if Johnny ever noticed that.

When the police interviewed me, I said we argued in the car. I said I got out and then Johnny drove away, mad and out of control. I don't want Johnny to sound like some kind of maniac. I don't want anyone saying things about him. They listed the cause of death as accidental, driving while impaired.

I'll never know what really happened at that last second. I keep reliving that moment when our eyes locked. Am I imagining that Johnny looked suddenly surprised to find us locked in a death embrace? Was it his love for me that made him swerve? Or was he punishing me by forcing me to see him kill himself? And if I hadn't run away—what then? What then?

School has started again. I walk through the halls and sometimes I hear someone whispering, "Wasn't she the one with the guy who—" I turn away and try to blend in with the walls. They guy who—what? I think. The guy who loved too hard.

Oh, I know it was not my fault. Rationally and logically,

it was not my fault. All it takes is a little reading and I can find the words for Johnny in the textbooks: fragmented personality, obsessive, addictive behavior, compulsive. I'm quite bright and I can figure out that it really wasn't my fault. I wish I hadn't followed his footsteps in the sand on that first day at the beach. Johnny being Johnny, there was no way to make it come out right in the end.

Jessica

Fall has come and gone. I see Mike around school sometimes, but we don't talk very much. He plays drums with Gary Vernon's band, he goes out with Melanie Phillips, and we hang with completely different crowds now. So I'm a little surprised when he calls me.

"Darren's in town. Tom's back for Christmas vacation, too, so I thought— We're getting together tonight and if you want to come down . . . ?"

I hesitate. "I'd like to see everybody," I finally say. I hadn't really expected to hear from Darren, but there's not been a word from Tom since Johnny. I thought we'd been really good friends. I wonder if he blames me. "How's Darren?" I say.

"It's the new Darren," Mike says. "Economics and computer whiz at Stony Brook. The future corporate wonder boy."

"And Tom?"

"I haven't seen him yet," Mike says.

"Okay. Sure. Where?"

"Three Deuces, around nine?"

"Oh." I haven't been there since—there is a long, awkward silence. Mike finally breaks it.

"Jess, we can make it Bruno's, if you want. Or someplace else."

"No, Three Deuces is all right," I say. Johnny will be there wherever we go. Four of us who used to be five. After the funeral, we all went our separate ways too abruptly. Maybe enough time has gone by for us to be able to share our memories. . . .

The Three Deuces is almost empty. I see them right away, at a table in the back. Tom and I hug hello, but it's by rote. I am shocked. He has become grotesque, blown up beyond obesity. Maybe that's why he's avoiding my eyes.

"What happened to this place?" Darren says. "I thought it would be jumping."

"The cops cracked down," Mike says. "The new management's keeping the high school kids out. Double-checking proofs and all that."

My ID still passes. My impeccable ID, courtesy of Johnny.

"Well, all the college guys ought to be back by this weekend," Tom says.

"I'd like to run into Steve Dunninger, you know the one that went to Wharton?" Darren goes on, about making business contacts and dean's list and MBAs and . . . He's as handsome as ever, and completely deadpan.

The Three Deuces is dimly lit and cold. There's a new bartender. I keep my down jacket on and I'm shivering.

"So," Mike is saying, "how're the bands at Stony Brook? You playing with anyone?"

"No." Darren's face looks tight. A beat and then, "I don't have time."

"But I just can't believe you don't—" I blurt.

"What's so hard to believe?" His voice is harsh.

Silence.

Quick change of subject. "Hey, Mike," Tom says. "What happened to your hair?"

Mike runs his hand over his head. "Yeah, I let it grow out. I was volunteering for Alexander Brady's campaign, you know, for the Senate? So I had to look kind of—normal." Mike grins. "Which, in my case, wasn't easy. Listen, the whole punk thing became trendy anyway. It was getting stupid. . . ."

"I'm not hearing right. You're not working for the establishment!" Darren is heavy on the sarcasm.

"Brady's a good man," Mike says. "I wanted to see him get in. A man like that could make a difference."

"But he lost," Darren says.

"There's always next time," Mike says.

"Wait a minute. I thought you were the messenger of doom," Tom says. "Anarchy was around the corner."

Mike shrugs. "So I've changed my point of view. There's no law against it, is there?"

Darren laughs and snaps his fingers. "Just like that?"

"No, not just like that." Mike's eyes are shaded. "You know, I was so busy condemning all the rot; I just forgot to be there for a friend when he needed me."

I wonder what he's talking about. I'm wondering if Johnny was the friend.

"So that forced me to think about where I was coming from," Mike goes on. "It's always easier to trash everything. More fun, less work. Listen, when I think of the things that struck me funny, things I actually *laughed* at . . . We were just cooler than cool, and out of control. No, there's got to be responsibility. There's got to be a moral center."

That's a conversation stopper.

Darren rallies. "What about you, Jess? What're you up to?"

"Not much. Just getting the college applications in."

"Where?"

"Tufts, Barnard, NYU."

"All big-city schools."

"That's what I want. That's if financial aid comes through." I want to reinvent myself in a big city.

"I was sorry to hear about your folks splitting," Tom says.

"Well," I shrug. "I guess it was coming for a long time." What made them finally do it? Kids growing up, last one off to college? Maybe the fallout from Johnny's passion made Mom alive to what she'd been missing.

"What are you majoring in?" Darren asks.

"I don't know yet. Math, maybe. I'm not sure."

"That's good," Darren says. "There's a lot you can do with math."

I can't think of anything else to say. Mike lights a cigarette. We were so intertwined last summer; the awkwardness between us is painful. There are four chairs around this table, and the ghost of a fifth chair. Which one of us is going to say his name first so that we can finally talk to each other?

The waiter approaches our table. A familiar, not-too-bright face, a holdover from the old management.

"Well, look who's here! Haven't seen you in here in a long time! What'll it be?"

Three beers, a large Coke for me.

"Boy, I still remember the night you guys played! The new owner's keeping the rock groups out, he says it makes trouble. But that was some night all right, you packed the place to the rafters."

"We did, didn't we?" says Darren. For a moment, his eyes light up.

"Business is dead now." The waiter turns to go. Then, over his shoulder, "Hey, where's that other kid? The one with the margaritas."

"Johnny," I say. It's the first time I've said his name out loud in months.

He goes to fill our orders and leaves us to our memories.

The new owner is making an attempt to decorate for Christmas. There are silver icicles hung over the bar, looking dusty and sad, leftovers from old holidays.

The drinks come and Mike holds his up. "To Johnny," he says.

"To Johnny," we echo.

"Sorry, Jess. This is rough on you." Since when was Mike so solicitous of my feelings?

"We can talk about him," I say. "It's all right. We all loved him, didn't we?"

"I grew up with him; he was like a brother," Tom says. "I miss him."

"I do, too," Mike says. "He stirred up excitement anyplace he went."

"He was a talented guy," Darren says. "He was one hell of a performer."

"I never knew anyone that died before, I mean, anyone our age." Mike runs his hands through his hair. "I still have nightmares about him."

Mine aren't nightmares exactly, I think. He doesn't do anything in my dreams; he stands still, white-faced, anguished, just staring at me.

"Sometimes I see someone that looks like him," Tom says. "Like from the back. And for a moment, I feel all this relief; I want to call out, 'Hey, buddy! You didn't really do it, did you? You'd never do that, right?' "

Tom grabs for his beer and takes big gulps.

"I didn't know he was that bad," Mike says. "He was very weird one night, but I didn't realize. . . . I should have told someone. I should have helped."

"He had a lot of weird nights," Tom says.

"What really did happen, Jessica?" Darren says. "Could it have been an accident?"

"I'm not sure," I say. "He turned the steering wheel toward the cliff. You could say that part was on purpose." The words hurt my throat.

"Suicide," Darren says.

"That's what I figured," Tom says. "I figured his dad covered it up."

"I'll never know for sure why he turned that wheel," I say. "I'll never know."

"Suicide. That leaves me mystified," Darren continues. "I couldn't get anywhere near that point for anyone. Not Barbara, not anyone. I can't grasp that level of . . . It's like there's something going on that I can't get a handle on. . . ."

I remember Johnny in performance, blazing, consumed with emotion. I suddenly flash that Darren, with all his cleverness, with all his technique, never had the heart.

"I felt bad about Barbara," Darren is saying, "but—"

"Most guys don't go and commit suicide because of a breakup," Mike says.

"I didn't *want* to break up with him," I say. "I mean, in the beginning it was good. But I had to. I felt like I was suffocating. I couldn't help it."

"You know, that's really stupid! What makes you think it was because of Jessica? It wasn't because of Jessica!" At first, I think Tom is defending me, and I'm grateful. But then he goes on, strangely adamant. "I didn't think he cared *that* much. Hey, I knew Johnny and I knew he'd get over it. It wasn't Jessica! It could have been anyone. As long as I knew him, he needed excitement. Something to engage him. She just happened to be there. It could have been anything. You know what I think? If that guy Ryan had taken us on, Johnny would have been okay. Johnny in the spotlight, feeding off all the—"

"Ryan didn't take us on, so what's the point?" Darren snaps.

"You'd think he'd at least have had the courtesy to contact you," Mike says.

"Well, he didn't!" Darren says. "What's the point of raking that over?" He is more short-tempered and withdrawn than I remember him.

"Maybe Ryan was a phony," Mike says, "too embarrassed to call because he had nothing to offer us. That's what I think."

I notice the cheek muscle working in Darren's controlled, expressionless face.

I sip at my drink and the ice hits my teeth.

"So what happened to Johnny?" Mike is running his finger around a wet ring on the table. "Drugs, drinking? How come some kids experiment and walk away unscathed—and others get sucked in? I wouldn't touch even grass with a ten-foot pole now."

"I still don't understand," I say. "I can't understand why it changed so suddenly. I didn't do anything and he started accusing me—like with Darren, remember that? Out of the blue."

"There's no use to this! No one knows what set him off!" Tom is tearing a napkin to pieces. "I want some pizza. You want to split a pie? How about cheese and anchovies?"

"No, I can't stay long," Darren says. "I have to see a guy about—"

"How long can it take for a pie?" Tom says. "And we're gonna have another round, right?"

The talk shifts—Bard has very small classes, Mike is trying to sell his car, Darren works part-time at the college bookstore, has anyone seen Dale . . .

I am in a bubble of isolation. Tom hasn't looked at me, not really, not once. I don't want to be at the Three Deuces. Not without Johnny. I miss the way he made me feel—everything heightened, even if it was haywire. The small talk washes around me.

"I have to go," I say. "It's a school night for me. North Bay's not on vacation yet and . . ."

We all say how great it was to see each other and we'll

do it again soon and there are the obligatory hugs. Mike offers to drive me home.

"I'd like to get together with you, talk to you some more," I tell him, "but I really feel like walking now. Thanks anyway."

"The physical fitness queen. Still running?" Darren says.

"Still running." Darren is so much a stranger tonight that I am momentarily surprised that he knows anything at all about me.

I walk up Main Street. The Chamber of Commerce has just strung neon wreaths above the street and some of the bulbs have blown out already. I am glad to be outdoors and alone. The wind against my face doesn't feel as cold as the air in the Three Deuces.

I don't know what's eating at Tom and Darren. I know what's making me cringe. What propelled me down the beach that day and straight into Johnny's bed was curiosity, song lyrics, media hype, "everyone's doing it"—all the wrong things. I deliberately chose him to be my expert, if unstable, guide. Cautious as ever—when I was sure of him, it seemed all right. It never even occurred to me that *he* could get hurt. I was in love with love, playing a role. I'm sorry. Johnny, I'm so sorry!

And I'm angry, furious. He could have killed me! I remember him haranguing me in one of those middle-of-the-night phone calls. "If I kill myself, it'll be your fault," he said. I was sleepy and I'd heard it before. "If you kill youself, it's your own choice," I said. "I don't control what you do." I ended a high school romance that was making me miserable. That's not a punishable offense. I wasn't responsible for his obsession. He made me the victim of it.

I go around and around, and I don't know what I think. We were too careless. Johnny's playboy veneer entertained us. He was a disaster waiting to happen and no one held out a hand. I see images of Johnny, many Johnnys, and the sadness seeps into my very bones.

I don't know what I think. It's still too soon to sort it out. Maybe Darren will find his way back to the music and Tom will find an antidote to suffocating in his own flesh. Maybe Mike has discovered that moral center he was talking about. And me—I hope someday I'll love and be loved, in an easy, uncomplicated way. But Johnny had grand passion, he was high drama careening crazily beyond the ordinary, and I wonder if something nice and normal will be too pale. Maybe it really was once-in-a-lifetime. Maybe a touch of insanity is required. I'll have to find out.

One of the decorations on Main Street is flickering, and then it recovers, bright, radiating a star-shaped glow.

I've turned seventeen and I'm alive and I'll have the time to find out.